Sara,

Enjoy the
chance.

Happy Reading

Rachel De Lune

Reminiscent HEARTS

RACHEL DE LUNE

©All rights reserved. No part of this book may be reproduced without written consent from the author, except that of small quotations used in critical reviews and promotions via blogs.

Reminiscent Hearts is a work of fiction. Names, characters, businesses, places, events and incidents are either the products of the author's imagination or used in a fictitious manner. Any resemblance to actual persons, living or dead, or actual events is purely coincidental.

Reminiscent Hearts ©2019 **Rachel De Lune**

Cover design by LJDesigns

Book design by LJDesigns

Editing by PAK and Roxane LeBlanc

Rachel De Lune on Social Media:

Facebook: www.facebook.com/racheldeluneauthor/

Instagram: www.instagram.com/racheldeluneauthor

Website: www.racheldelune.com

"There comes a point in your life when you have to stop reading other people's books and write your own."

Albert Einstein

ACKNOWLEDGEMENTS

This book is for my readers.

To everyone who has picked up one of my books and read it, reviewed it, shared it with a friend, thank you. From the bottom of my heart.

Hugs.

1
LILY
16 YEARS OLD

"Hey, Earth to Lily!" Louise shouts from across the table. I try and remember what she was saying to me and fail. The noise of morning break in the sixth form common room drowns her words.

"Sorry, what did you say?"

"What lesson have you got next?

"Psychology, why?"

"You sit next to Jake in class, and I was hoping you could speak to him for me. See if he wants to come to my brother's party on Saturday?" Her sickly sweet request makes me want to vomit. Louise isn't what I'd call a friend—more like someone who hangs out with the girls I do consider friends. Unfortunately, my actual friends never see the Louise who treats me like a lesser mortal.

"I didn't realise you were having a party?" I force a smile to stay on my face.

"Um, yeah. Didn't I tell you? Of course, you can come along, but will you speak to Jake?"

"Sure." I groan. Her overly glossed lips grin at me before she leaves our table and heads into the thick of our fellow students who mingle around for the twenty-minute break.

"Sorry, I thought you knew about the party," Charlotte whispers to me, sympathy explicit in her big wide eyes.

"No. You know she only talks to me if there's something I can do for her. I doubt Jake will mind me asking."

"Why don't you just say no to her?"

"Are you serious? To Louise?"

Charlotte giggles at my shocked expression. "Okay, I take your point."

The bell blasts, cutting through the common room mêlée, and we all move in the direction of our next class.

My heart pounds a few times against my chest as Jake walks straight past me to speak to one of his friends. "Hmm." I exhale quietly in disappointment. Of course, he walks past me. I never warrant a public display of friendship in front of his peers, at least not in this social setting. Jake is happy to talk to me in class, or if he needs something. But to notice me, smile at me across the room once in a while, see me for me—Lily Hill? Never.

My stupid girl crush isn't going anywhere, and it's starting to piss me off. No matter how hard I try to forget his stupidly gorgeous good looks, or his naughty grin, or his slightly rough voice, I can't. Every time he opens his mouth to speak my body relaxes into him. Sometimes I have trouble remaining focused on what Ms. Young is saying. I've been addressed in class for not paying attention, and I feel the biggest fool in school. I can't afford to get distracted. I have to work to keep my grades up rather than drift off into another daydream that stars Jake.

Jake is the ultimate prize for any girl—every girl. Thick brown hair, hazel eyes which shine with mirth and a body that looks years older than he is. He's the bad boy you love to like. He has an air of mystery about him, as if he's untouchable in school. He never gets into serious trouble. I suspect that's due to his quick wit and charm more than his behaviour. His silver tongue can talk him out of any situation. His social circle is vast but never close, and he doesn't conform to the usual calendar of drunken parties. On the few occasions I ventured to one, he would arrive late, show his face and leave with a girl in tow. His apparent ease at picking up whoever he chose propels him to 'king' status amongst both the guys and the girls.

I take my seat in the classroom and try not to watch the door for Jake to amble in. I fail, as usual. He pulls out his seat next to me and sits back in his chair. I bite my lip and take a deep breath before turning to face him.

"Hey, Jake. Are you going to Louise's brother's party at the weekend?" The words stream together in a rushed sentence I only just make out. He looks up from his phone and smiles at me.

"Louise who?" He raises his eyebrow as if waiting for me to explain further.

"Louise Cole? Blonde, short hair...can't get enough of her pink lip gloss?"

He still holds a dark, vacant expression which makes me wonder if he's listening to a word I'm saying. I want to snap my fingers in front of his face, but I could never be that rude.

"Will you be there?"

His question stuns me. "Umm, probably not. Louise only told me about the party to ask you. I don't think it's really my thing."

He shrugs. "Well, I haven't made plans for the weekend. If I don't get a better offer, tell her I might."

"Fine," I huff out. Jake can be a real bastard when he wants to be. The romantic inside of me believes we are bound to each other and our friendship just needs to be nurtured for it to blossom in to something more. Just when I'm on the verge of giving up on having anything to do with him, he makes just enough effort to reel me back in. It's times like these when I feel I should have my head examined.

Our back and forth has been the same since we were thirteen. I'd stayed late at school to finish some homework at the library. I was rushing to leave before it got too dark—I hated walking home in the dark. There were hardly any street lights on our road and reaching our house gave me the creeps.

I saw Jake's dad waiting along the lane next to the school. Andy, his brother, went up and high-fived his father before getting in the front seat. Jake was chasing to catch up. I'd expected his dad to greet him the same way, but it was nothing alike. His dad smacked him around the head and yanked the bag from his back. He opened the backdoor for Jake and then threw his bag in after him before slamming the door.

At that moment, my feet refused to take me home. They were glued in place. Jake's sad eyes locked with mine and I couldn't look away. All I saw was a little boy who wanted to be like his older brother. His idle stare gave me the impression he wasn't surprised by the greeting. Like he was resigned to it. His eyes didn't let me go until the car sped off, and I could only make out the red tail lights. I never saw his dad again, but I saw plenty of his brother. Jake stayed close to him around school until he left to go to university.

We've been sort-of friends ever since. I never ask him about his family, and he never volunteers any information. It's as if the evening never happened, yet it's etched into my mind so deeply I always think about it when I see the harsher side to Jake. Those few moments had tied me to Jake, and although the tenuous threads may have frayed, they always make me go easy on him when I really should give up and never speak to him again.

"Have you got your essay finished?" I change the subject, wanting to get back to surer ground.

"Essay?" he asks, again looking for me to explain.

"You know, the one assigned last week comparing the multi-store model of memory and the working memory model?"

"Looks like I've got a piss-poor memory, huh." He wiggles his eyebrows humorously, and I'm right back to loving him again.

I turn away and bury my head in my hands and try to balance

out my own mood towards Jake. The lesson is over with no other wisecracks from Jake, and I head over to the other side of the school for my last lesson of the day.

"Hey, Lil, wait up," Jake calls after me, and I freeze. He waits for the steady stream of students to thin around us before going any further. It's my turn to look expectantly at him.

"So, you have a better offer for the weekend than what's-her-name's party?"

"No, I just don't think it's my thing." I pull my books into my chest and inch my feet towards my next class. As much as I want to keep talking to Jake, I don't want to be late. I keep my eyes away from his, not wanting to get trapped in them. It's a constant hazard I'm susceptible to. I'm sure he can see everything I feel if he will only look a little harder at me. As no other guy in school has ever shown me any attention, I'm under no illusion the first one will be Jake Stewart. My feet start toward the science block. Jake walks beside me a little way. Sometimes, on the occasions when Jake was close to acting like a normal friend, I felt as if he was waiting to tell me something. It never transpired though and like all the other times, he peels away and turns back in the opposite direction. No 'bye' or 'see you later', but then, that isn't Jake's style.

He's absent for the rest of my day, but he's never far from my thoughts. It's getting tiresome, but that's what my life is all about, isn't it? Studying hard, being a good friend and getting through to the end of A Levels?

Biology is over before I even plug my brain into gear. I'm sure I'd regret not paying attention when I struggled with the homework assignment. I file out and walk home along the quiet country road. Our school is on the outskirts of Bristol, out in the sticks. Only a few villages surround it. "Lily, wait up. What's up? You've been lost in your own world all day," Charlotte calls after me.

"Oh, sorry, Charlotte. I don't mean to be." I keep up my steady walk toward home. It is Wednesday, which means I have to get home and head straight back out to work. At least waitressing will give me a rest from thinking about Jake.

"So, are you going to come to Louise's this weekend? You've not been out with us for ages. It will be fun, and there will be all those older guys there, too. You never know, someone might take your fancy."

"Somehow, I doubt that. Besides, I'm pretty sure Louise only invited me so I'd speak to Jake. You know she doesn't really like me."

"So? She can be a bitch, but that doesn't mean you should miss out. Come on, the rest of us are going. It will be fun. Puhleese." She pulls on my arm, desperate for me to agree.

"Okay, but you're coming over to mine first. I'll ask my dad to take us. There is no way I'm going on my own."

"Deal. Eeee!! We'll have a blast, I promise." She lets go of my arm, and we start back home again.

"So, will Jake be there?"

"You as well?" I inwardly groan. *Is there anyone who doesn't like him?*

"No, no, no. He's too scary for me. I was just wondering, you know, for Louise."

"Scary? I wouldn't call him that."

"Well, no, he's fine with you. He talks to you, or at least, his version of talking. You should see how he looks at some of the other guys. It's like he's holding in all this rage, and he's just waiting to let it loose on someone."

"I've seen his dangerous look."

"Yeah, well he's too offhand and distant for my liking, not that he isn't gorgeous."

"Do you want to come over on Sunday to go over the biology assignment?" I steer the conversation away from Jake. Despite the fear everyone can see what I feel for him, I'd kept my feelings secret and hidden as best I could. I didn't want to be the source of the bitchy gossip that was rife amongst some of the girls. Unless the ruling princesses deemed you 'popular' and 'pretty', you would never survive being turned down by a guy like Jake. I'm not popular, although I get on with most of my fellow students. Charlotte is the pretty one. I'm the dependable and hardworking friend who has never been asked out. This is common knowledge to my peers, and the likes of Louise uses it for ammunition whenever she can.

"Alright, but you know you'll do fine. You always do."

"Stay at mine on Saturday, and we can study Sunday." I know what Charlotte's like. Studying will go out the window any chance she gets.

"I suppose that's a good plan."

"Can we get home now? My shift starts at six."

Charlotte threads her arm through mine and marches us home.

JAKE
16 YEARS OLD

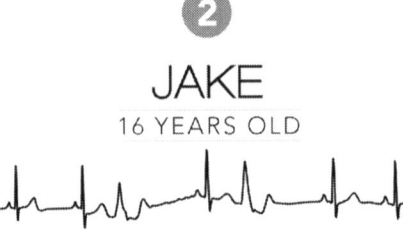

"I'm home!" I call and wait for any response.

As usual, nothing comes. When Andy left for university, Mum and Dad seemed to forget me altogether. I've always lived in his shadow, but now it was a miracle they remembered I still live here.

When Andy was still at home, at least I saw my folks. Now, they come and go as they please, as if they'd forgotten they should still be an influencing factor in my life. Didn't bother me. I've grown up expecting nothing less. At least they leave me alone.

I grab a drink from the fridge and slump in front of the TV. I scan through the channels and try to let the mindless noise numb my brain. It's always the same after I see Lily. I can't get her out of my fucking head, and that does wonders for my piss-poor mood. I'm stuck in my own fucking groundhog day.

The next day, I focus on whatever Ms. Young is spewing out in psychology and pretend not to feel Lily's presence next to me. What pisses me off more, is she didn't ask me what was wrong, if I am alright, or why I haven't said a word to her. I want her to talk to me, but can't show that to her or anyone else. And the most frustrating thing, she knows I won't want to talk and lets me do my thing. Which, more often than not, consists of being a total fucking bastard. She isn't scared of me like some of the other kids at school. She's just her usual sweet self. I spend way too much time being angry. First, my anger was directed at my parents, then at Andy. Living with my family and becoming used to how they treat me has turned everything bitter. I am the complete opposite of Lily and hate being so fucking attracted to her.

She is so sweet. Her huge, innocent eyes, beg me to kiss her every time she dares to look at me. And God I want to. I want to punish her lips with mine, take her innocence and devour her. It is a fucking miracle I can still sit next to her in class. The images of her body, hot and sweaty writhing under mine, consume my mind and drive me around the fucking bend.

My first fuck was Yvonne—and I haven't stopped fucking since. Yvonne had a thing for my brother, but when he lost interest, she turned to me. Having an older brother who could pass for your twin didn't seem so bad when Yvonne was shoving my dick into her sweet heat. She made the most obscene noises as I jacked my body against hers and it lit something inside of me. Sinful cries, sweat-coated skin, and the best orgasm I'd ever had, sealed my fate. I fucking love sex. Not the pretty, gentle, make-love kind. I went for the hard, rough, dirty as hell type that made my cock throb and my blood come alive. Fucking was the only time I felt good, the only time I felt like me. Everything else was for show.

Nothing will ever change at home. Mum and Dad don't give a damn about me when they have their number one son. According to them, I'll never amount to anything. If you hear something often enough you believe it, and it makes me fucking mad. I'm never going to be good enough for them—never good enough for Lily.

Sex is the outlet for my anger—that and anything physical. But, Lily is a constant frustration. I shift in my seat as images of her sweaty, well-fucked body come to mind. *I need to get laid.*

Sex gives me some relief from anger I can never escape. I don't care if the girls enjoy it. I spend no effort to make fucking them "special" and we sure aren't on any god-damn date. Those girls are fifteen minutes where I think with my dick—fifteen minutes where I picture Lily's face, Lily's sea-blue eyes, Lily's fucking cries.

The bell rings, and I'm out the door before I do something stupid like fist Lily's hair and kiss her fucking senseless. That's only the start of my fantasy and it has me racing to my locker. I dump my books, grab my kit and head to the changing room. I will run home and attempt not to smash something on the way. Running is the easy resolution to the rage that always curls, ready to unwind in my gut and wreak havoc. I will fight the pavement with my feet and punish *the concrete* for the way I feel. Each thud of my trainers ricochets through my body and delivers the sliver of satisfaction I seek.

The sweat drips from my spent body by the time I arrive home. The soles of my feet burn from the pounding and remind me of just how hard I'd run as I collapse on my bed. My reward is I keep in shape and can focus on something other than Lily-fucking-Hill. If she isn't going to Louise's party, I will do my thing. Pick up whomever is the opposite of Little Miss Perfect.

We have a love-hate relationship. Ever since our stolen scene back when we were kids, she's held a piece of me and she doesn't even realise it. I'll never forget her look of disbelief, of shock and horror. It was as if her innocence rejected seeing my dad shove me into the car like a stray dog. He'd violated her picture of how parents treat their children.

I hated that she saw me that night, but we'd never spoken about it. I should have been embarrassed she'd seen me, but it wasn't like that night was a one-off. That kind of behaviour from my father occurs regularly. I am always an afterthought and live in Andy's shadow. I'd spent a few years playing at being a good son. Didn't make any difference, I was still yelled at or ignored. So

I do what I want. No one stops me, so why should I stop myself? My one exception is Lily Hill. She still has the same wholesome, innocent eyes which struck me that night, and whenever I see her, I have to work very hard to keep her innocence front and centre in my mind.

I grab a quick shower while the house is still quiet. Unfortunately, Andy is sitting on my bed as I come back into my room.

"Hey, little brother." He lies back, lounging like he owns the place.

"What do you want?" I run the towel over my hair and toss it towards the laundry basket, hoping it will hit the mark and not the floor.

"That's no way to greet your favourite brother. I came back for the weekend. Thought we could hang out and earn some brownie points with Mum. I was going to offer you a treat, but now I'm not so sure."

"Get to the point, Andy. I'm not in the mood." If I were a bastard, I'd learnt it all from Andy.

"Then I have the perfect solution. Come party with me tonight. I'm sure Yvonne will be there if you want to let off some steam?"

"That was a one-time fuck. I'm not bothered," I grumble at him. I can't deny the thought of sex with her makes my dick hard as nails.

"I'm pretty sure you're not going to turn that kind of pussy down, hmm? Think about it. Me and a couple of other mates from uni are heading out in a few hours. Tag along. Or not." He saunters out of the room, his elitist attitude hanging from his every move.

I finish drying off, but it doesn't shift the blood pumping to my cock. The run is a distant memory.

Four hours later we head up the drive to some random house in town. A friend of a friend was hosting this little party. Andy had an open invitation, and right now, all I want is to drink a couple of beers and sink my dick into Yvonne.

Andy's nearly four years older than I am and in his second year of university. I idolised him when I was younger. His shiny halo dulled as we grew older and I realised I'd always come second to him with Mum and Dad. Didn't stop me benefiting from the spoils that came from having an older brother. Despite the difference in our ages, we were evenly matched; both just over six foot, wide solid frame—swimmer's build. It certainly helps with the girls.

Andy has always succeeded in everything he does. He has the skills and the drive to succeed academically and socially. Because he has done so well, Mum and Dad see him through rose-tinted glasses. They turn a blind eye to his partying. He gets his cake and eats the fucker, too. My work ethic focuses on something much darker, and it takes every ounce of willpower I have not to punch Andy's lights out. He knows exactly what I'm struggling with and is happy to remain the perfect first born. He shoves my face in everything he has that I don't, including a blond who had to settle for the younger brother.

There is nothing natural or genuine about Yvonne. She's a poor Barbie impersonator with her fake blond hair and fake tanned skin. I've no doubt our paths will continue to cross until she loses interest in my brother. Until then, I'm not going to turn her down. Her smile oozes satisfaction as she sees us enter the main room. It's pretty obvious Andy is having his own fun with her as he makes a bee line for a pretty little thing, ensuring Yvonne sees.

One of the guys we came in with hands me a beer and I chug half the bottle before Yvonne crosses the room to me. There's no doubt about her intention. She cosies her body up against mine, her skin-tight top straining to contain her tits. My eyes take their fill before I look up and think about wiping the smile off of her pink-stained lips. Her talons trail down my chest, and I snatch her hand away before she reaches the buckle on my belt. She led the way the last time we hooked up, but I've learned since then. My hand grips her wrist, and I yank her to follow me upstairs to find an empty bedroom. It's still early which ensures two things. We will get some privacy, and I won't get sloppy seconds.

I slam the door behind us and pin her against it. I drop the bottle from my hand and smash into her lips, destroying her sickly sweet lipstick. My hand yanks her leg up to wrap around my waist, and I pull her thong to the side. The little slut's already wet and creamy. I finger her cunt, being as forceful as I want and listen to the soft cries she makes. It's not enough. She's far too quiet, so I shove another finger deep inside and am rewarded by her sharp gasp and moan. Her gasps are what I want from her. I work my fingers hard and listen to her growing sounds of pleasure. My mind relaxes and despite the lewd situation, I feel a calm descend.

"Keep your legs spread wide for me," I growl. My hand leaves her thigh to grope her tits. I pinch and squeeze, all the while, digging my fingers into her heat. She does as she's told and lets me have my way. The louder she gets, the better I feel. Her cries make a sexual lullaby. She screams as I finish her and I feel her pussy clench around my fingers. My dick is rock-fucking-hard and impatient to be in on the action. I pull my fingers out of Yvonne and man-handle my cock out of my jeans. I roll on some protection before sinking deep inside her waiting pussy. I anchor my hands in her hair and thrust into her with hard, sharp movements. The noises that come from her throat are fucking delicious. Throaty and loud, they pump me up higher than anything. I can't help myself, I pound into her, each thrust lifting her foot off the floor. She only enjoys it more.

This is what I want to do to Lily. I want to wipe the innocence from her eyes and fill them with pure sex. I want to strip her back to her base instinct, and I want to make her scream. My tongue wants to lick her skin clean of desire. I want every dirty fantasy my inexperienced mind can conjure, and I want it all with her. I want to tear her apart and have her love me for it.

My head rears back as I climax, thinking about Lily. *God, I'm a bastard.*

3
LILY
16 YEARS OLD

"You look great, Lily. Come on, come on." Charlotte practically bounces off the walls as we get ready.

"Alright. What's the hurry?"

"Nothing, I just don't want to be late."

"Liar. It's a house party. We can't be late. It's fine. You don't have to tell me."

"Is your dad alright to drop us off? Do we need to get a taxi home or will he come and get us? I haven't asked…"

"Slow down, Charlotte. Dad is fine with taking us and will pick us up as long as it's before midnight."

"Midnight?" She looks shocked, as if she was expecting this to be an all-nighter.

"Yes, come on. I'm happy if you don't want to stay over. You can stay as late as you want and then go home, but you need to let me know how you're getting home. I don't want to leave you there on your own."

"I won't be on my own, silly."

"You know what I mean. Promise me?"

"Fine, I promise."

"Are you ready girls?"

"Just coming, Dad!" I call down to him and usher Charlotte out of the room.

"You know where we're going right?" Mum eyes me over the

book she's reading on the sofa.

"Have a good time, girls."

"We will Mrs. Hill. Come on Lily, we're going to have a good time. Okay?"

"Okay," I mumble and head out the door.

Half an hour later, we're outside of Louise's house. A booming bass deafens us before we even enter the house. A few shadows mill about by the front door. I run my hands down the front of my jeans. Charlotte insisted on skinny jeans, stating they were the only way to go, so I forced my legs into two tiny pipes of fabric. She'd lent me a pretty pale blue top. The material is sheer but not risqué. I use a black blazer jacket to keep the spring chill at bay. Charlotte is gorgeous with her womanly figure and lush hair. The boys always follow her with their eyes as she walks past. She could take her pick, and I'm very thankful she hasn't turned into one of the 'princesses' with her increased popularity.

We edge ourselves through the people outside and open the door to the house. Thumping beats attack us as we push through into the hallway. The music comes from the living room, and Charlotte leads us in that direction, letting her body relax in time with the insane bass.

A few faces from school pass my vision, but I don't see any from our group of friends. Charlotte makes a loop of the room. The sofas and furniture have all been pushed to the side to make a makeshift dance floor. We exit back the way we came and head toward the kitchen. The sweet smell of mixed drinks and beer wafts in the air as we walk through. Bottles, cups, cans and rubbish, fill every square inch of surface space. The people in the room look a lot older than we do. I try to shrink behind Charlotte, feeling well out of my depth. She takes no notice and pulls me with her as she goes in search of a drink. She fills two plastic cups with a mix of coke and vodka and hands one to me. I take a tentative sip and nearly choke on it. Charlotte certainly needs to work on her ratio of coke to vodka. The mixture strips my throat, burning through my senses, and my eyes water as it hits my stomach. I try and squeeze the drink back onto the kitchen table, but Charlotte just glares at me.

"It's one drink, come on," she shouts over the music.

"Just one." I hold up my index finger, making sure she can't misunderstand.

At the far end of the house, there's another room serving as a hub of activity for the make-shift party. An enormous flat screen TV plays music videos while music blares out of a smaller sound system. The room houses several sofas and chairs all pointing towards the magic box on the wall.

A familiar guy is sitting on one of the leather sofas furthest from the door. For a moment, my heart squeezes in my chest as recognition startles me. It's not Jake, although he looks the spitting image of him. If Andy is here, Jake will be too. My heart starts to flutter at the thought of seeing him. My initial excitement chills as I know what he'll be doing. His routine is cast in iron. He picks up trashy girls, the bitchy, name calling ones who I hate even more because he likes them. It's gutting to see the guy who stole your heart against your will, flaunt every girl he is currently playing with in your face. I'm sure he isn't. It just feels that way. His fuck-bunnies are just another part of our friendship I've had to swallow.

"Hey, I don't see anyone here we know. Are you sure the others are coming?" I try and pull Charlotte back out of the room. It's quieter here at least, the dull rhythm of the music letting the words of our conversation reach our ears without having to yell.

"We just got here. You've not even finished your drink. Come on, Lily." She ignores my feeble attempt to bail and doesn't let my lame complaint deter her. She pulls me after her as she continues to search through the house. We end up outside on a large decked area which opens out onto manicured lawns and designed beds of flowers and foliage. A group of girls are sitting on the garden chairs, and to my relief, I see a few of our friends.

"Hey, Claudia, Jenny," I offer as we approach.

"Look who made it after all." Louise approached from the side, the contempt in her voice clear.

"Yes, thank you," I mumble, wishing I could say something other than thanks.

"Did you at least get Jake to come?"

"He told me he'd see what he was doing." I leave out the part about a better offer. No matter how she talked to me, I couldn't find the words to sass back at her. That wasn't who I was, no matter how much the words burned to get loose.

"Did you say who was inviting him? I hope you didn't try and set this up for you?" She looks down her nose at me as if she couldn't imagine a world where Jake would find me attractive. I already knew that and didn't need her to rub my face in it.

"Don't be a bitch, Louise," Charlotte warns Louise, but all she does is roll her eyes.

"He said he'd come if he didn't get a better offer. His brother's here so I'm guessing he is too. Seems like he wasn't in a rush to come to find you, though..." My words would have been much more satisfying if Louise had actually heard any of them. It seems someone had caught her attention, and she scampered off. Straight into Jake. *Perfect.*

I swiftly take a seat in one of the chairs and pretend I don't see him. It wouldn't be like he'd come over or anything. He always acts like I am invisible when we do see each other like this. I push Jake to the back of my mind—another chore I am very used to doing—and turn to Jenny.

My drink is finally empty, and I remain firm in my decision

not to drink any more. Charlotte, on the other hand, hasn't listened to the same advice. She has downed at least three other vodka cocktails and is now looking a little green. After settling in with the others, we had a good evening. A few guys had come over to chat with Charlotte, Jenny and Claudia. I wasn't sure if they were from our year or people who Louise's brother had invited.

It's a little after 10:30 p.m. and I need to venture inside to find the loo and grab a glass of water. "Hey, I'm heading inside. Does anyone want a drink? Aside from Charlotte, that is?"

"Hey, no fair. I'm… fine."

"Sure. I think you need the water more than I do. Come on." I ease her from her chair, and we head back in.

The noise from the house had escalated since we arrived. There are people everywhere. A hot wave engulfs us as we open the back door and try to push through the crowd. It's insane. People are crammed in and spilling out of the front door. My sensible head sees disaster written all over this.

"Come on. I need to find the bathroom before we get you some water." We reverse our roles as I keep hold of Charlotte who has started to sway. I look around the hallway and try to spot the bathroom. There are only a few people on the stairs, so I start in that direction, but I stop. As I look up, Jake stands at the top of the stairs, leaning against the side bannister. Louise is draped over him. I have the perfect view of both of them.

I take a gulp of air and hold it in my chest, determined the balloon of air will protect my heart from breaking. Jake's hand is holding her bum, pulling her into him. I don't think she could be plastered any closer. Her hands stroke his chest. She's all over him and not being at all subtle about it. I take it all in in a blink. I see the sly look in Louise's eyes and the hard set of Jake's jaw. My eyes flutter to clear the tears forming, but I can't tear them away.

As if he can feel me watching, Jake turns his head and stares straight at me. His eyes, devoid of all emotion or warmth, hold mine. The little lost boy from my memory is nowhere to be seen. His eyes aren't mischievous or playful. They are harsh and cold and my stomach crashes to the floor. My heart misses a few beats.

We stare, locked in each other's sights. My eyes focus on Jake, and I can't break free. He turns his head to Louise, and with his eyes locked on mine, licks the side of her face before he claims her mouth and kisses her deeply.

I push Charlotte back down the two steps we'd climbed and head straight for the door. I pull the phone from my pocket, text my dad and ask for a pick up right away.

"Hey, what's going on?... Lil, I don't… feel so good." Charlotte bends at the waist and heaves into the bushes. I focus on my friend, and it distracts me from the pain piercing my heart. I should have learned by now some things will never change. Jake will never see me as anyone other than a casual friend. I am nowhere near his league. I shake my head in despair. I'm hopeless. I still feel the way I've felt since the moment our gazes locked three years ago. My heart belongs to him, so I do what I've always done. I plaster a smile on my face and pretend my heart doesn't break every time I see him with someone else. But this time was different. This was the first time he was a complete dick about it. It felt like he was kissing her just to hurt me, to make his point even clearer. I'd never measure up. He'd never choose *me* to kiss. With an unsteady breath, I shove my tears down. I refuse to give him the power to hurt me more than he already has.

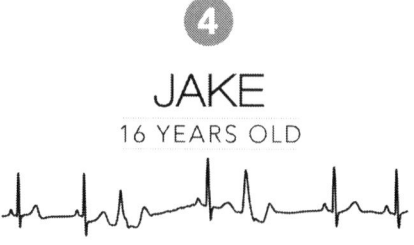

JAKE
16 YEARS OLD

*A*fter the so-called party Andy dragged me to, and my encounter with the horny slut, Yvonne. I thought I'd reciprocate and bring him along to the girl's house Lily mentioned. I can't remember her name, but that never seems to be a problem. It's her brother's shin-dig after all. So far, it's all pretty desperate. At least I can relax and not worry about seeing Lily here. It isn't her thing. Anonymous hookups and free booze aren't what the lovely Lily is all about.

Andy kicks some younger kids out of the game room and a few others tag along with the big boys. Honestly, this is all a load of lame shit anyway. A couple of the lads from school have already passed me a couple bottles of beer. I down them and toss the empties before going in search of this Louise girl. If she couldn't be bothered to ask me here herself, I'd find out if she was worth any of my time.

I have a hard time identifying her as I can't distinguish her from the other pouty, blond girls who seem to sidle up to me as soon as I'm in reach. My tour of the house winds up outside, but I wish it hadn't. Clad in skin-tight fucking jeans which make her arse look too fucking hot, Lily is talking to some bimbo. The wanna-be Barbie catches my eye and heads straight to me. Of course, Lily notices me too, but thankfully ignores me and goes to sit down.

"Hey, Jake. Thanks for coming. Fancy a drink?"

The words register, but I haven't stopped watching Lily. She's eased into a chair as far out of the way as possible. She's hidden away amongst her friends, which is the best place for her. Out of trouble and out of my mind. *I fucking wish.*

"Jake, are you listening to me?"

"Not really, but hey." I turn and walk back into the house, but little Miss Barbie follows. It seems my piss-poor behaviour isn't enough to put her off.

Barbie sticks to me all evening. She is quite efficient at fetching beer. I've had way more than I should. I'm a fucking wreck. This girl is getting closer and closer to me, and all my eyes can look at are her tits.

"Want to go upstairs?" she offers with a sultry grin that does nothing to entice me.

"Sure."

She leads the way and all but drags me up the stairs and into her room. "How do you want me, Jake?"

"How about on your knees and sucking my dick." I push her head down until she gets the message. Her hands fumble at my fly, and I can't help but snigger. Anxious hands grip my dick and pull it to her lips. I'm only half hard for this girl, so I imagine Lily on her knees for me, her big doe eyes staring up at me, wanting to please me. That image revs things up, and my dick is practically begging for this girl to deep throat me. If she's interested, she should know the drill.

I let her run her lips over my cock, but she's clearly never blown a guy. I grab her head and force her mouth up and down on my dick. The protests and her slight struggle amp up my orgasm. Saliva seeps from her lips and the slurp and moan of her mouth fire my come down her throat. She swallows and gags as I keep her head against me, but she doesn't push away from me. "You could use more practice, whatever your name is. I've definitely had better."

Barbie-bitch sits back on her heels and looks up at me with confusion clouding her eyes. I am amazed there is anyone in the school who doesn't know I'm a complete bastard to girls—happy to take and use them as I saw fit. If she thought she could change me, she's mistaken. Not even Lily can change me, and I'll never cross that line. I couldn't live with myself if I ruined her, no matter how much I want to.

I tuck my spent cock away and head for the door.

"Is that it?" she whines.

"What were you expecting?"

"Well, a bit of affection, maybe you'd make love to me? We could hang out?"

"I'm not in the mood to fuck anyone tonight. And I don't hang out."

"You do with Lily."

"She's none of your business."

"Well at least spend the rest of the party with me."

"You can keep getting me beer." I open her door and walk back out onto the landing. A few of Andy's friends have made it upstairs, and I go over to say hi. Miss Barbie-Bitch follows and wraps herself around me as if that's what I want. I look over the bannister for an escape route only to be stopped dead by Lily. She looks up at me with hope in her eyes. I watch pain replace longing as she takes in the wandering hands of Barbie-Bitch.

My anger should be quieter in my mind. I'd fucked it into submission with Yvonne, and the blow job at least got me to finish. I should be calm. One glance at my ultimate fantasy and I'm ready to storm down the stairs and punish her for coming here—punish her for the way she stands out like a fucking beacon amongst all the easy girls and punish her for getting inside my head. I'm fed up, tired of seeing the longing and desire in her eyes when she looks at me. I'm tired of always watching her and wanting what I see, only never to act on it.

I move my hand around the slut's hip and pull her in tight. Keeping my eyes on Lily, I lick Barbie's cheek, staking a claim in the most obvious and crude move I could make. It's the worst thing I've ever done to Lily. I've deliberately hurt her. She watches and I see the blow to her as if I had physically struck her. She runs.

Barbie nuzzles at my neck and draws my attention back to her. She's moving her lips up to mine. "I don't think so." I push her back and storm down the stairs. I search the game room for Andy.

"Come on. I'm leaving," I shout at him.

"And? I don't remember having to follow you, little brother. If you want to leave, then leave. Thought you'd have your pickings here, I mean, there are some sweet chicks."

"Do what you like." I'm pissed off and want to get out of here.

I leave the party and stalk home. The buzz from the alcohol is long over. Seeing Lily has vaporised the relief the blowjob had given me. The night air holds a chill that wakes up my body, and I break out into a run. It's only a couple of miles to get home, so I keep my mind busy by running and not remembering the haunting pain I saw cross her eyes. No, not going there. Maybe this would help her move on, help her realise I'm not the guy for her. She should stop torturing me. *God, I'm a bastard.*

5
LILY
17 YEARS OLD

"Why do you always leave things to the last minute? You've known about this forever." I eye Jake in frustration.

"Lily...come on...you know I plan as little as possible, and besides, I have you to bail me out." His grin walked the line between cocky self-assurance and conciliation.

"And please remind me why that is?" I ask in jest, yet I did need an answer. Thankfully, for my sanity, my heart had stopped melting into a puddle whenever he walked into a room. I think it took a pretty big hit last year at the party, and I've been much better at hiding my feelings—letting things just be. My change in attitude seems to have eased our random friendship. There are still the awkward silences and the pitiful attempts at being friends in school, but we see each other more now than we used to. Things are finally stable between us. I'm not ready to give up, and Jake is trying, in his own way. We are good.

"Because I'm me, and you're you, and that's just who we are."

His answer is a little more philosophical than I was used to. His sense of humour had decided to show itself recently. It's a good side to Jake, less intense. He still is the gorgeous heartthrob every girl hopes to get a shot with. He still does his own thing, which I'm very sure I don't want to know about. He's still all mysterious and seems to keep everyone hooked. But he is nicer to me. Some girls would think it a good thing—a step in the right direction. For me, it re-affirms what I've always known. Jake will never see me as anything other than a friend, and that's okay.

I concentrate on the psychology textbook in front of us and will my heart to stay quiet. I don't want him to see I still have feelings for him. I've been so good at hiding them.

"Are you going out with Charlotte again?" I ask without looking up.

"Why do you ask?" No humour in his response.

"Well, she told me you had a good time. Plus, she didn't come into school in a terrible mood, so I'm guessing it wasn't a complete disaster."

"We were at the same party. Doesn't mean we're dating. Come on, Lil, leave it."

He scowls, apparently not liking my line of questioning. I find being open about the girls he sees, and there are a lot, helps. Plus, it proves a useful disguise. What sane person would do this to themselves?

"Are you sure this is the final part of the assignment?" he grumbles to me.

"Yes. Coursework needs to be completed tomorrow."

"Great. I'll see you in class." He grabs the books off the table and hurries out of the library.

"Jake, wait…" But he doesn't hear—or chooses to ignore me.

I pack up the rest of our books and head home, firing off a quick text to Jake.

Sorry. Hope you get everything sorted. See you tomorrow.
Lily

When Charlotte caved and told me she fancied Jake a few months ago, I wanted the ground to swallow me up. It was the hardest thing I'd done to pretend I was excited about it. She's convinced she's going to stop his bad-boy behaviour and be the one he will call a girlfriend. My heart suffered in silence, bound by determination, as I focused on my smiles. I still wished to be Jake's girlfriend, but I know he'd never call anyone that—at least no one from school. He still acted like his brother and paid no heed to any consequences. Not that there were ever any for him. I'd be grounded for a month for even putting a toe out of line. I can't risk that.

A huge part of me can't wait to get away and spread my wings at university. I'd get to start fresh, and hopefully, my heart would give me a break from Jake. I *could* meet someone. Jake will never be mine. I'm fine with that.

JAKE
17 YEARS OLD

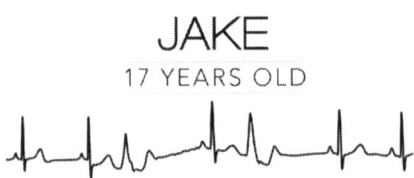

Grrr! She is driving me so fucking crazy.

Two months after watching as I broke her heart the first time, I gave in. The silent treatment just tore me up. I couldn't take it any longer and broke our silence. I missed her. I fucking missed her and so I tried to be a decent human being and started talking to her again. At first, only in class. It was tolerable. I kept the focus on school work.

I'm still fascinated by her. Nothing has changed. But, it's as if she's hiding something. She keeps to herself, stays within her safe group of friends, always works hard. The rest of my life is pretty fucking shit, and I never realised how much Lily balances that out. Being this close to her isn't working either. And now, she is asking about the girls I'd potentially go out and fuck before dumping their asses and moving on. It was insane.

Charlotte was at the last party I went to. Sure, she was fit and pretty, but she reminds me of Lily. No fucking way I was tapping that. Girls needed to be as opposite of Miss Lily Hill as possible, and still in spite of every effort to control my imagination, it's always her I fuck.

I have one more year to get through. Then I can head off and make something of my life, show Andy and my parents just what hard work looks like and be rid of Lily Hill. I'm hoping 'out of sight—out of mind' will work in my favour.

The buzz in my pocket means she'd just texted. I can read her like a book. She wants to check in after the way I left. I'll speak to her later. Right now, I need out of my head. I head home and change into some running gear before ducking back out. Summer is fast approaching, and it has been dry for a while. I hate running in the rain. It's fucking depressing.

Running is now the best solution to reeling in my lust. It didn't mean I stopped pulling easy girls when I was out—they ask for it as much as I need it. The more sex I have, the more I want. Dirtier, harder—I even make sure I have Yvonne's number in my phone. She is local to Bristol and is always happy to oblige. I couldn't care less about her history with Andy. There is less guilt when I screw her. I know I can be as nasty as I need to be. She knows what I like and doesn't hold back in showing me just how much she enjoys the rough treatment.

My phone vibrates a second time, and I curse under my breath. Is it too much to ask to be like all the other guys at school? To date the hot girl, worry about exams and earn some money for a car? Instead, I get parents who think they can buy my affection with an over-the-top gift after treating me like shit the rest of the time and an older brother with a nasty fucking streak who is happy to grind my face in how much better he is than me. My anger should have gotten me in a lot more trouble than it has. So far.

I push my legs harder, welcoming the burn as it overtakes my other senses and chills out the hum of rage in my brain.

Less than a year before I can escape, only a couple of months when you consider school ends for exams early. I can make it. I just need to cut the faint tie of friendship with Lily Hill—the tie I'd failed so miserably to sever in the past. It will take something brutal. I need to make her hate me. *God, I'm a bastard.*

6
LILY
17 YEARS OLD

"Charlotte, please, let me study. I have to get a B or better in biology or I won't get my place at uni. I know it's easy for you, but I need to study."

"Oh, come on. You work harder than anyone else in our class. You'll be fine. Besides, all you do is study. You need to have a bit of fun as well. Exams start in a few weeks. One night isn't going to ruin your chances." Charlotte certainly has her pleading look rehearsed and perfected. Despite her growing popularity, she didn't let it go to her head. She was always a true friend. Unfortunately, her interest in Jake hasn't lessened. I'm sure he will be at whatever party she's twisting my arm to go to.

"If I come to this, will you help with my revision notes? You can do this stuff in your sleep."

"Sure. But you have nothing to worry about."

She leaves my table in the library, and I go back to my books in peace. I never saw the appeal in going to all of these parties. They are all the same and usually ended with someone in tears. I've never shed the many I've accumulated within me. I don't want to show anyone that Jake is my biggest weakness. To the outside, we are just friends, and I am happy I can pull that off.

Are you going to the party on Saturday? Charlotte will be there. Lily

I fire off a quick message to see if I need to suit up and put my mask on at this party.

If I go, doesn't mean I'll hook up with Charlotte. I wish you wouldn't play matchmaker. Jake

Ok, I won't. See you there. Lily

You're going?! Jake

I've been known to go to parties. Lily

I know. I just didn't think you'd come along. Jake

Don't you want me to go? Lily

See you there. Jake

Great. I turn back to my biology textbook and groan at the thought of getting anything else done tonight. I slam it shut and grab my folders and head for home. I'd pulled back my waitressing shifts because of the revision I needed to concentrate on, so I didn't have to work. One shift a week was enough, although I did miss the money. My savings account wasn't growing as rapidly as I'd hoped. I knew university was going to cost a fortune. Mum and Dad are footing some of the bills, but the more I can save now, the better. I still have the summer to work, I suppose.

For once, the party doesn't look like it will be a total disaster. Nearly everyone from school is here. We are crashing some guy's massive house. The kitchen is the size of the whole downstairs of my house.

Charlotte is dressed to impress, and we all know who her effort is directed toward. We meet Claudia and Jenny here, but no one has spotted Jake. Not that I am looking for him. Really... I'm not.

A group of guys walk past our gathering in the kitchen. They are the first people I don't recognise from school, although one of them stands out. His height makes it hard not to notice him, but I continue to stare. He's gorgeous. Jet-black hair and a square jaw that makes him look like model material. My lips tip up into a smile I have no control over and my stomach does a flip as my eyes refuse to look anywhere but at him. He chooses this moment to look my way, and our eyes meet. My cheeks flush the moment they do, and I turn away in embarrassment. No other guy had ever been able to catch my attention. It had always been Jake.

"Hey, who's that? He's totally checking you out." Jenny whispers in my ear.

"I have no idea and no he isn't."

"Oh, hun, you really wouldn't spot a guy looking at you if he stood right in front of you and stared. Please take our word for it. He is."

I ignore her comment and stare at the interesting plastic cup filled with coke in my hand. My eyes avoid everyone and their unwanted attention. I will my cheeks to cool, but I can still feel the tingle left behind by the rush of heat.

The smile on my lips is still there, and for the first time in a long while, I feel lighter. Excitement tickles my spine. My whole body erupts in goosebumps and a shiver wisps over my skin.

"Hi, I'm Tim."

"Hi, Tim. I'm Charlotte. This is Claudia and Jenny."

I lift my head from my drink and stare at Charlotte.

"And this is Lily."

I turn to Tim, and my lips stretch wide into what I hope is a nice smile.

"Hello, Lily. Nice to meet you."

Dark blue eyes smile at me with genuine interest, and the heat creeps back up my neck and onto my cheeks. He's flanked by a couple of guys who look half pissed off, half bored. My eyes scatter everywhere other than back to his face, and I turn to put my drink back on the kitchen counter, desperate to find something to do other than stand and drool.

"So where are you boys from? I don't recognise you from St George's." Claudia breaks the tension.

"We're from City Academy. Jeff is a friend of Mark's, so we came along," Tim replies, and I find the courage to look at him. The faintest sprinkle of freckles cover his cheeks, making him look adorably sexy, and I stare for just a little longer.

"Can I get you another drink, Lily?" His lips move, and I do my best not to let my cheeks flame anymore than they had already.

"Sure, just a coke, please."

"You got it." He moves to the make-shift bar set up in the kitchen and gives me the space I need to breathe.

"Oh my god, he's so cute. He's totally into you, and, you like him. I can see it all over your face. You should get his number," Charlotte prompts.

The girls all close in and fire statements at me, talking over one another.

"Shh, calm down. Just…" I try and exert some order.

"Lily, one coke." He passes me the plastic cup, and I let our fingers touch. I smile at him, and he returns it, making me feel ten feet tall. I've never been glad I'd made an effort to come out before. Now, I wanted to squeeze Charlotte in the biggest hug ever.

"This is Craig and Adam." Tim points to the two guys who have been hovering in the background. They both do a sort of nod thing towards us and go back to looking around the room.

"So, guys, fancy a dance? We girls have been here for too long without enjoying ourselves," Charlotte pipes up, and I close my eyes in horror at her suggestion.

I can't dance, and the thought of trying to jerk my uncoordinated body to the music in front of Tim makes me want to smack her. I take back the mental hugs I gave her just a moment ago.

To my utter horror, Tim replies, "Sure. Lead the way."

Charlotte grabs my hand and pulls me out of the kitchen and across the house to the lounge. A bank of overstuffed sofas split the room. They create a private area much more suited for my disposition, but we walk past them and join a few people dancing at the far end of the room. The open area spills out onto the deck in the garden where others laugh and enjoy the warmth of the spring evening.

Charlotte turns to us and starts to move her body in time to the music of Jason Derulo. She still has hold of my hand and isn't letting me get away with being a wallflower. I try to mimic her moves. It's more of a body bounce and sway than dancing, but I don't think I look out of place as my eyes scan the dancers.

Jenny, Claudia and Tim gather around us and glide into the rhythm. I fight the draw of my eyes to Tim's but finally give in and our gaze meets. His eyes tell me he likes me. For once in my life I feel sought after and an unfamiliar thrill courses through me. His body moves effortlessly in time with the beat, and he edges closer in towards me. His hand reaches out and slides right around my waist. My instinct is to tense, but I push it away. The hum of excitement hasn't left my body since I first glanced at him and I want to enjoy this.

We spend the next few hours dancing and laughing among our little group. Even Adam and Craig have joined with us. It's been the best fun I've had in ages, and I feel on top of the world. A warm glow spreads throughout my body, and my cheeks ache from smiling so much.

My phone vibrates in my pocket, and I pull it out.

I'm outside. Time to come home love. Dad.

No! My face crinkles in a frown, and I lift to look at Tim who's watching with interest.

"Everything alright?" He leans into me, and a shower of tingles fall over my body.

"I have to leave. My dad's here to pick us up."

"That's a shame. Can I give you my number?"

"Um, sure. I'd really like that." I hand him my phone, and he saves his number. He hands it back to me, and I tap the call icon and phone it. Now, he can call me... if he wants to. As the thought pops into my head, my stomach flutters with hope he will call.

I tap Charlotte on the shoulder and signal we need to leave. She shrugs but starts towards the front door. I give a little wave to Tim, but he grabs my hand and walks me out. As he reaches the door, he stops us. He towers over me—he must be over six foot— and smiles.

"It was really nice to meet you."

"You too. I had fun." I'm shocked to realise that I mean it. I had fun.

"Good."

Butterflies tickle my stomach, and my limbs feel shaky. No guy's ever kissed me before and right now, that's all I want him to do. My eyes look up into his and I hope I don't look as desperate as I suddenly feel. My heart races and I'm afraid I might hyperventilate.

After what feels like the longest few seconds of my entire life, he dips his head and brushes his lips across mine. My body trembles and I reach out to hold onto his arms for support. He pulls back a fraction before kissing me again, gently caressing my lips. His slow and sensual glide has my mouth opening as he traces the seam of my lips with his tongue. The kiss is soft and slow and I let the sensation wrap around me, blocking out everything else. It's over before I want it to be and I stand, stunned, looking up at Tim.

"I'll speak to you later." He plants a chaste kiss on my cheek before he slips back into the room where he left his friends.

Oh my god, did that just happen? I touch my lips in amazement and turn to race after Charlotte to tell her I've just been kissed by the most amazing guy.

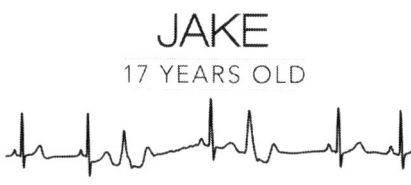

JAKE
17 YEARS OLD

The party is already in full swing as I walk through the door. A few guys greet me as I make my way through to the kitchen to grab a beer. I know Lily will be here, so I came late. If she's here to drink and have fun, there's no way I want to witness it. I find it hard enough to keep my head clear of everything Lily Hill at the best of times.

She's my own personal curse. She's my best friend, who I purposefully steer clear of because I don't trust myself enough to be around her on our own. I've lived with the constant battle of trying not to give in to my feelings for her for a long time now. Yet she manages to make me feel guilty without even trying. Or it is my own guilt eating away at me? After all of the shitty things I'd done to the girls I'd slept with and then left, I would have expected some pang of guilt. Zip. Nothing. Then all Lily has to do is look at me and I feel like the biggest git. She doesn't even realise what she does to me.

I grab a beer from the counter in the kitchen and head out the back door. Night had drawn in, despite the long sunny day. I take a seat next to a few guys from my psychology class who are sitting on the decking. From this position, I have a perfect view of the two main rooms of the house. And a perfect fucking view of Lily dancing with some stranger.

I stand abruptly.

"Hey, watch it, Jake."

I look down and realise I've tipped beer all over… this kid's lap. "Sorry, my bad."

I sit back down and wrestle the possessive fire bolt that just struck my chest. I have no fucking right to be jealous. I could have Lily if I want. I know she still has feelings for me. She tries to hide it, but every time those big tempting eyes look at me, I can see all the emotions she keeps inside. She's never told me how she feels, never spoken about it with her friends, from what I can tell.

It's been our mutually kept little secret. All the way through school.

Until this fucking minute, as I see this guy pull her in closer and whisper in her ear. Her innocence screams at him. I bet he can even smell it on her. That fresh flowers in spring scent that never seems to leave her. Another thing that drives me fucking crazy.

The guy seems to have a couple of friends with him. I don't recognise either of them.

"Hey, anyone know who those three stooges are?"

"No, they aren't from St. George's."

I settle in and watch. The shadows shroud me in darkness and keep me hidden. I must be a masochist because it's fucking misery. Lily is sweet, kind and laughing like she doesn't have a care in the world. She's breathtaking.

She stops dancing and pulls out her phone. I look at my watch and notice the time. Midnight is her usual pick up time. The guy follows her as she and Charlotte leave. I see them in the hall through the next window along, and I don't think twice about getting up to see just what this guy's intentions are.

My view into the room is obscured, but there is no missing the kiss he gives Lily. The fucking kiss I'd always wanted to give her. After she rises up into him and returns his kiss, the rage inside gets the better of me, and I smash my bottle on the floor. I ignore every pair of eyes that are now on me and march right back into the room.

Prince-fucking-charming returns with a shit eating grin on his face.

"You! Don't you ever fucking hurt her, you got me? If you do, I'll make your life a fucking misery and be happy to do it." My hands grip his shirt collar as I spit the warning at him.

Several pairs of hands try to separate us, but they have no fucking chance.

"Relax, man. I'm not going to mess with her." He has an inch or so on me in height, but I more than make up for it with brawn. "What's she to you? You her brother?"

"No. Just watch yourself. She's too fucking good for you." My heart stampedes in my chest as I lay down my warning. I release him and leave the room. I'm pumped and ready to rip someone apart. Every sense is heightened, and I need to get out before I do something fucking stupid. I turn and realise everyone is staring at me. It's eerily quiet as the music has suddenly been turned off.

I do the usual and ignore everyone and leave through the garden and around the side of the house. *God, I'm a bastard.*

LILY
18 YEARS OLD

The summer is nearly over, and I hate it. The end of school and exams are bad enough. It was only a few months ago I was looking forward to going off to university. Now, I don't want to leave everything I know behind. My world has completely shifted, and it's unsettling.

Tim is coming around later. He's a big part of my about-face change in attitude. I don't want to leave him even though we'd only been going out a few months. We fit together so seamlessly that I feel incomplete without him. How are we supposed to survive being separated by university?

I flop back onto my bed and pull out my phone. I've seen Jake only a handful of times before exams started. I keep texting him, checking he is all right, seeing if he wants to go for a drink. He has been unusually quiet.

Hey, you can't ignore me forever. It would be good to see you before uni!?

I don't expect a response straight away, but I'm hopeful our strange friendship means more to him than a convenience through school. Although, I'd never felt convenient before, more like the opposite. No matter what, I didn't want to let Jake disappear from my life. On some level, his friendship confirms I'm good enough for him. As much as I don't want to feel that way, I can't help it. I've been in love with him for years—and unrequited love sits heavy in my heart.

Tim helps lessen that ache. He is wonderful. Kind, compassionate, patient. I don't get to see him at school, but that only means we have lots to catch up on over the weekends. We study similar subjects and biology suddenly seems much more interesting. Charlotte offered to help me with revision, but I want to spend time with Tim. He makes it hard to concentrate at times, but the exams go well. My grades secure my spot to study physiotherapy at Birmingham—only a two-hour journey to Cardiff, where Tim is studying.

We haven't discussed what would happen in a couple of weeks. We've both been wrapped up in each other, spending a lot of time just hanging out, listening to music, messing around with friends. He fits right in with the girls—at least Charlotte, Claudia and Jenny. His friend, Craig, has a pool in his back garden, and we've certainly made use of it. The summer has been fantastic and the more time we spent together, the more my feelings for him grow. But real life is creeping up on us, and I want to stop, put everything on pause and stay in this time forever.

We can go out tonight. I'll pick you up. Jake

Oh, for god's sake.

I can't tonight. I have plans. Can we do it tomorrow or another day? Lily

With him?

Yes, with Tim. Lily

I huff out my frustration and set about deciding what to wear for tonight. Tim hasn't told me what we are doing, only that he wants to make it special. When I think about the possibilities contained in the word 'special', my skin breaks out in a sweat. We haven't had sex—at least not all the way. Despite how relaxed he makes me feel, how sexy and wanted, it's a big step for me. We certainly haven't held back the few times we were alone at his house. He played with me, fingered me and kissed me until I was gasping for air, but hadn't made me come yet. He was gentle and tender when he touched me. I felt precious to him. Sex was the next step for us, I could feel it.

Being close and intimate with Tim helped to keep my mind on him rather than Jake. Jake had played a huge part in my fantasies. I always imagined Jake to be the guy I'd lose my virginity to. No other guy has ever come close to catching my interest or showing any in me. Tim changed all of that. He sees me, likes me for who I am. He'll be my first. The excitement that accompanies my nerves gives me confidence—this is the right thing. He is the right guy.

I've already consulted Charlotte on what to wear. The autumn weather hasn't set in yet, and the warmth of the brilliant summer still clings to the air. I want to go for a cute top and jeans, but apparently my 'go to' outfit isn't something to wear for a special night. Charlotte had made specific instructions I should wear my blue skater dress, my hair down and my ballet pumps. She said I'd look sexy and cute. I don't see it myself. Awkward and plain is what always stares back when I look in the mirror. Sure, I have nice eyes, nice hair, but I am plain. I don't shine like some of the other girls. Tim noticing me at that party had me beaming for days. I'd been waiting for Jake to *see* me for years. I was startled to feel Tim's eyes on me. It was as if he woke some part of me waiting deep inside my entire life.

I drag myself from my bed and find the dress I'll be wearing. If I think about tonight or Tim for much longer, I will drive myself crazy with second guesses.

Two hours later, I am sitting on the edge of the sofa downstairs, waiting for the doorbell to ring. Finally, the bell chimes and I rocket out of the chair.

"Bye, Mum! See you tomorrow," I call out and race to the door. I open it and duck out before Tim can say anything.

"Hi, ready to go?" I ask, smoothing down my hair.

"Sure. Come on." He reaches for my hand, and I feel instantly lighter as he encases mine in his.

"Are you taking me out for dinner?"

"Actually, yes." He smiles.

"And anything else?" I ask.

He opens his mum's car door for me, and I scoot inside.

"There doesn't *have* to be anything else. I don't want you…"

"No, I want there to be something else." I look at his concerned face and wish I could calm the nerves that insist on shaking my body. "Please, I want tonight to be special. You know, for us. I'm ready." I blink my eyes and battle the urge to feel shy about this conversation. If I want to have sex with him, at least I can have a conversation of sorts about it.

"If you're not ready, I understand, I don't want to pressure you."

"No, I do. I am. Trust me. I want this with you. We're ready. Please. In fact, can we skip dinner?"

Tim looks as shocked as I feel. But all of this waiting and thinking about tonight isn't helping. I don't think I can sit there and eat knowing after we finish, we'd go back to his house and have sex. I couldn't take that.

"Come on," I giggle to him. "Let's skip to dessert." We both crack into laughter at my ridiculous pun, but Tim seems to be in agreement.

We head over to his house in relative silence, but at least now I know what's coming.

His house is empty when we arrive. He holds my hand and leads me up to his room. Each step sends my heart into a faster flutter until I'm sure he must be able to hear the beats.

"Where is your family?" I croak, nerves tangling my tongue.

"Out. They won't be back until late. We're alone."

I sit down on his bed and clasp my hands in my lap. The anxiety I'm suffering drowns out the bravado I felt earlier. My eyes roam around the room and avoid looking at Tim who hasn't moved from his position by the door. My legs cross and wrap around each other as I try and fight off the nerves. My stomach feels like a battleground for the butterflies trapped in there. It's sickening, and I can't calm my heartbeat, even with a few deep breaths.

Finally, Tim walks over to me and sits down. The bed dips and I lean into him. His hand cups my face, and he places a soft kiss on my lips. His touch grows firmer, and he tilts his body into me. His strong arms come up around my back, and I feel his fingers work at the zip on my dress. I fight off the tension that stiffens my body and let the zip expose my skin to him. Until now, we've played things pretty safe. Sure, the kissing has turned pretty hot, and I know he finds me desirable, but our clothes have stayed on.

I kiss him harder, wanting to reach the point where I'll relax. I want the nerves to stop.

"Lie back, baby."

I do as I'm told and let him peel off my dress. I push off my flats, so I'm left in just my underwear.

"You're gorgeous, Lily."

I force my arms to my sides, though I want to cover myself. I look up at Tim, and it's the first time I've really looked him in the eye tonight. He strips off his shirt and jeans. He lies back, and his finger begins to trace the side of my face.

"You know this is my…" I start.

"I know. Don't worry. I'll take care of you." His warmth envelops me as he rolls over me. He presses his body into mine, and the connection sets all sorts of sparks buzzing through me. His kisses grow firmer. No longer teasing my lips, they trail down my throat and my chest. My breath catches and I feel dizzy from the attention. My whole body tingles and breaks out in a wave of heat.

Tim's hands grow bold as he explores the plains of my body beneath him. I relax under his touch and the tremors cease as he slides his hand under my knickers and opens me up. His fingers dip inside of me, sending my stomach into summersaults. He continues to touch me like he's done in the past and my heart speeds up. This is something I want. With Tim.

His fingers grow in confidence and I widen my legs, feeling weak and hot all over. He leans down and plants a kiss on my stomach and he trails them up my torso. I want to squirm under his attention. It's so intense, I feel completely taken over by him.

He rolls away, and I watch as he puts on a condom.

"You ready?" he asks with a wide grin on his face. My voice is stuck, so I nod. He eases my knickers down before settling himself between my legs. I try and swallow back the rising panic at the thought this might hurt, or I won't like it. My brain knows the first time isn't going to be all hearts and explosions, but I want it to be special. I've given my heart to Tim. He's the one who cares for me and wants to be with me. I fight my mind not to drift off and think of Jake. I want to show Tim how much I care for him.

He stares down at me, and I get lost in his soft, kind, loving eyes. I feel my heart swell as I realise he feels the same for me as I do for him. He pushes gently at my entrance but doesn't break eye contact. The stretch stings and I take a deep breath as a slice of pain cuts through the emotions boiling up inside of me.

"Please tell me you're alright, baby?" Tim drops his head and breathes against my neck.

"Yes, don't stop." Tim starts to rock into me, the pace gentle and caring and the pain eases to a warm ache.

His breathing begins to quicken, and he bites at my neck, sucking the skin between his lips. I feel my whole body quake and a rush of heat pools at my core.

"God, Lily, you feel good."

My body burns like a furnace as Tim speeds up further. He's still careful with me, but I also feel desired and wanted, and it turns me on. My body relaxes. Intoxicating joy washes the nerves away. I lean up and capture his lips, kissing him passionately. My hands explore his back and dip over the muscles that bunch under my touch as he moves inside of me.

We get lost in each other. All I can feel is Tim and the emotions he's pulling from me. My body begins to shudder as a rush of heat swamps me.

"Lily, I'm gonna come," Tim pants, and I hold him tighter. My tongue slides over his lips, and he moans into my mouth. He pumps hard for the first time and it sends a jolt of electricity through me. My stomach coils and tightens and I want to explode.

"God, Lily!" Tim cries out as he releases. He continues to slide in and out of me as all the muscles in my body contract and a wave of pleasure bursts from my core and I come.

He drops down on top of me and wraps me in his arms. An eruption of emotion bubbles up inside of me at what just happened. My heart rejoices that I found Tim—considerate, loving, patient, Tim. He's made my first time everything I thought it wouldn't be. If this had been Jake, he'd be pulling on his jeans and leaving about now. But maybe I've read too much into tonight? Maybe it doesn't mean the same thing to Tim as it meant to me.

"Is this a goodbye thing? You know, before we go off to uni?" I ask, scared I got this all wrong.

"What do you mean?" He pushes back up so he can look at me.

"Well, we're both going in different directions. I know I wanted this, but I'm hoping it's not a goodbye."

"No, no. I don't want this to be goodbye. I don't want us to be apart." His hands run through my messy hair, calming my skittish thoughts.

"Really?"

"Really. I know we haven't talked about it, but I don't want us to split up, Lily. You're cute, funny, kind and sexy as hell. You drive me crazy. I want to do things right with you. I wanted this to be special for you because it's special for me too." He looks away for a moment before returning his eyes to mine. "I love you, Lily."

Tears sting my eyes as I look into his and see the truth of his word. His smile lights me up, and I squeeze him as hard as my arms can manage. "I love you, too."

JAKE
18 YEARS OLD

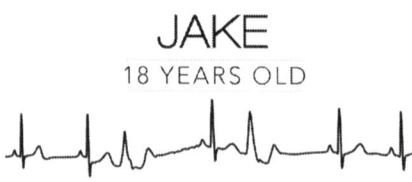

Come on stranger, just a coffee? Lily

I throw my phone back on the bed and stomp out of my room to grab something to eat. It has been a few weeks since I've seen her, and even then it wasn't to talk to her. I've been doing a pretty good job of ignoring her. It fucking stung that she picked her new boyfriend over me the other week. I know that's stupid. I have no rights over her. I'm barely civil to her. She tolerates my shit and seems to understand me, and I give her nothing in return. She still texts, still tries to get through to me. A small part of me still wants that from her, and that makes me weak.

I pull a few things out of the fridge to build a sandwich. The house is empty, no surprises there, and I have no other distractions to keep my mind from plaguing me with thoughts of Lily. I've been seeing a lot of Yvonne. She and the gym have kept me out of trouble—if you can count it as that. Two more weeks and I'm off to London.

I take the make-shift lunch upstairs and grab the phone off the bed.

Coffee later today. 2pm. Jake

Sure, I can make that. It will be good to see you. Lily

I wish I didn't feel the same way. No matter how hard I try or what I do, I want to see her.

I walk into the coffee shop and scan the seating area. Lily is sitting, twiddling her hair looking just as sweet as always. The flowers on her top contrast with the grey clouds and drizzle that has set in. She doesn't have a drink yet, so I make my way over to her.

"Hi."

"Oh, hey, do you want a drink?" she asks eagerly.

"Sure." We both make our way to the counter. There's an awkwardness about it, as if neither of us are comfortable. She's never like that.

"A hot chocolate, please and a…"

"Black coffee, cheers." We place our orders and take the drinks back to the table she picked out.

"So, what have you been up to? I haven't seen you much."

"Not a lot. Had a few things to sort after the results but it's done now."

"Oh, like what? You never did tell me how you did. I hardly saw you at school."

"I did well. I'm going to University College London now. Undergrad law."

"What, wow. Congratulations. You must have aced your exams." Her smile transforms her face to a picture of beauty. Pure and innocent and so fucking beautiful. It's clear she's really happy for me. It doesn't make it any easier to distance myself from her.

"Yeah, I start at UCL the week after next."

"That's great. I thought you were good with staying in Bristol?"

"I think a change might be best. A clean break."

"How does Andy feel about you going away? I know you two are close."

"He's a big boy. He'll be fine." In truth, I haven't told him or my folks yet. This is something I want to do to prove to my family I can make something of myself without them. I am never going to win the favourite son competition, so why try? I've spent the last three years screwing around and by some miracle managed to come out on top. I don't need my so-called family. The sooner they are out of my life, the better.

"I'm leaving next week for Birmingham. Tim's off to Cardiff."

My hands clench my mug at the mention of her boyfriend. I hate the idea she has a boyfriend. "You two going to do the long distance thing?"

"Yes, well at least try. We both feel the same way, so it's not like I'm forcing him to or anything."

"Sure."

"What, you don't think it will work?"

"I didn't say that."

"You didn't have to." She turns away, a knitted brow and sad eyes replace the joy that lit up her face just a moment ago. She takes a sip of her chocolate and leaves a smudge of the sweet stuff on her lip.

"Hey, I'm sorry."

She looks up at me, and I can't help but slide my thumb across the corner of her mouth, taking the chocolate with it. Her pupils dilate as I stare into them, and I curse myself for the stupid move. I'd always kept my hands to myself with her. No matter how fucking hard it was, I refused to give her any indication I had feelings for her, or what I wanted to do to her. Her eyes can't hide what I know she still feels for me, despite her boyfriend. Will I ever be free from this girl? "I need to get going."

I stand and break the connection growing between us. I need to leave before my imagination and anger take over. Lily isn't to be touched. That has always been the rule. It fucking hurt.

"Wait." She grabs my hand to stop my escape. "I don't want you to leave and never speak to you again. Promise you'll stay in contact?" Those fucking eyes again, searching mine for…

something.

"I'm not sure, Lily."

"I don't want to lose you as a friend. Please, Jake. Promise me."

"We'll see." I pull my hand away and leave. *God, I'm a bastard.*

LILY
20 YEARS OLD

Come on Jake it's Christmas. I've not seen you for ages. Just one drink. Lily

God, you don't give up, do you. Coffee at our usual place. Jake

JAKE
21 YEARS OLD

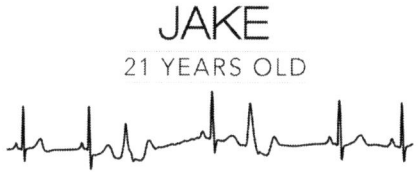

I'm home for the summer. Are you? I can't believe we've finished. And don't even think about getting out of meeting up. You've been crap. Lily

I had no doubt you'd be nagging me. I'm still in London, but I'll be home next week. Jake

Good, I'll look forward to seeing you. Lily

LILY
24 YEARS OLD

"Hey, baby, have fun. I'm hoping Jake doesn't bail on me. I'll see you later." I call from the front room to Tim.

"Sure, I won't be long."

"No rush, see you later." I kiss Tim as he heads off for football.

We have beaten the odds and have just moved into our own house. High-school sweethearts who made it through uni and are now living together. It doesn't happen all the time. We both agreed Bristol is where we want to live. I've just started my intensive care rotation at the BRI, and Tim is working for an agency in town. The one bed flat is small, but it's ours.

I am surprised Jake agreed to a meeting. We've only seen each other a handful of times over the last couple of years. In fact, it had been immediately after uni when we'd seen each other last. No matter, I don't want to give up. I hadn't made friends easily at uni. I'd spent a lot of time visiting Tim rather than building the friendships others around me seemed to be doing. I love Tim, and I didn't want to risk jeopardising us for a couple of parties with friends I might not keep in touch with.

Charlotte is the only other friend from my past I still contact regularly. Through everything, we still see each other, regularly text and make time for each other. I know I was forcing the point with Jake. Ever since the meeting at the coffee shop before we went off to uni, I've been pushing to keep the friendship alive. Perhaps it's because he was my first love, or I still wondered *what if* when I was feeling blue. Part of me feared I would never stop wondering. Does anyone when it comes to first loves?

I can't shake the weird connection I've felt for him for all these years. As long as he continues to return my random text messages, I won't give up. I don't want to give up. As fleeting as he now is, Jake is part of my life. So many of my memories from school include Jake. That doesn't make a lot of sense, as he'd bruised my heart on many occasion, but I always forgave him. Jake was part of who I was growing up, and no matter how much Tim has pushed Jake out of my heart, I can't forget him.

I jump in the shower quickly—it had been a busy shift, and I need to feel human again. I sweep my hair into a messy top knot and dress in some leggings and a flowery top, not that I had any other types.

The buzzer goes, just as I pick up my phone to remind Jake that he promised to see my new place. I press the intercom to let him up and wait. I still get a flutter in the pit of my stomach before I see Jake. I am totally in love with Tim and beyond happy, but there is something about Jake I just can't shake. It is more than just being attracted to him. Like a tiny sliver of my heart would always belong to him, and it woke up when he was around.

I open the door and wait. The Jake who walks towards me is nearly unrecognisable. He's bulked up, his natural size honed spectacularly. His eyes look darker and stubble covers his jaw. I shake my head and smile in welcome, ushering him in.

"Come in, come in." He hands me a bottle of wine as I close the door.

"Hi." His greeting sounds tentative like he's on edge.

"Thanks. Do you want a glass or I have a bottle of beer?"

"Beer would be good."

"The lounge is straight through. I'll just grab us a drink."

I scurry off to fetch drinks and return to find Jake in the leather armchair in the corner of the room. The apartment isn't huge. A tiny kitchen and bathroom but the living room is a nice size with room for a dining table.

"I'd offer to give you a tour, but there isn't much left to see."

"No, worries." His smile is faint, but it's there beneath the scruff. I hand him his drink.

"Cheers."

"Cheers." I take a swallow of wine and curl up on the sofa closest to his position.

"So, you need to fill me in. What have you been doing since uni? It seems like forever ago."

"Yeah, it's been a while. Well, I'm working as a lawyer in a firm in Bristol, but I'm moving back to London next year."

"Oh, congrats. Are you enjoying it?"

"Yeah. It has its perks. How long have you been here?"

"Only a few months. I'm working at the Bristol Royal Infirmary at the moment. Tim's working in the centre, so it suits us."

We've always been able to fall back into a fairly easy banter, despite how long we'd left it before meeting up. Something about this time felt different, though. It's harder. It had been the longest gap between our meet ups. We'd both been off living our lives, and there is only so much you can do to try and keep a friendship alive. Perhaps we'd left it too long? I push the thought aside, refusing to give up on the sad-eyed boy staring at me from the back of his car.

"How's your brother and family?" I had only seen Andy a handful of times but I'd always gotten the impression they were close, despite what I saw of Andy and his dad that night.

"I've not seen them for a while, but they're good. Andy is engaged now."

"Really, wow. And what about you? Any girlfriend?"

He looks at me and smirks. "No. No girlfriend."

"Hey, I'm back!"

I hear Tim call from the hall. "Oh, hey. I wasn't expecting you home so soon?"

"No, the game got cancelled, so I thought I'd come and say hi." Tim looks over to Jake and nods. He leans over the back of the sofa to give me a kiss.

My cheeks blush at the public display in front of Jake. It is stupid, but I can't stop it. "Okay, I'll just go and put some food in the oven. Jake, did you want to stay for dinner?" I ask.

"Um, sure. Why not."

"Great." I jump up and head toward the shoe-box of a kitchen. I pull a few ingredients from the fridge. Fajitas are quick and easy. Peppers, onions and chicken all make their way to the counter, and I begin to dice.

I have to stretch to reach the pan on the top shelf, cursing Tim for putting it back in the wrong place.

"Here, let me help." Jake's hand rests on my hip as he leans over me to pull down the uncooperative kitchenware.

"Thanks."

"Look, I think I'm going to give food a miss. It's been nice to catch up. You look really good. Happy."

"You sure? It's no trouble."

"Yeah. See you around." Jake turns around to leave. I follow him to the door. My heart pounds in my chest. Something is off, and it's weighing in my stomach.

"Jake, stop. Why do I get the feeling this is goodbye?"

"Because it is." He smiles and looks at me for the first time tonight. I know what he's doing. He's been pulling back for years. I've just refused to let it happen.

"You know what I mean. I feel like I'm not going to see you again. Ever." A wave of sorrow hits me as I think about never seeing Jake again. I know we had an unconventional friendship, but I consider him one of my best friends. He means more to me than many of the people I see every day. I'd grown up with him, been in love with him. It is strange considering our distance the last few years, but I can't just dismiss our past. I won't let him do this.

"If you're in London, come and say hi."

Our gaze locks for a fraction too long, and I feel the familiar connection we've had since we were kids.

"Take care." He plants a rushed kiss on my cheek and then closes the door behind him before I can stop him.

Tears prick my eyes and my vision blurs as they tumble down my face.

"Hey, did I hear the door?" Tim meets me in the hall.

"Um, yeah, Jake decided he'd give dinner a miss." I dash the tears from my face before I turn around to look at Tim.

"Hey, stop that. What's wrong?" He bundles me up into his arms before I can swipe the pesky tears away.

"Nothing. I'm just being silly."

"Nope. Try again."

I wait until the emotion is free from my throat and take a deep breath. "I don't think I'll be seeing Jake again," I whisper. Scared to say it too loud in case it comes true.

"Ever? You know Jake, baby. He does this. He goes quiet, then you catch up and then he goes back to being quiet."

"This time it feels different. I think it's different this time. I can't explain it. God, I'm sorry." I lean up on my tip-toes and wrap my arms around Tim. "I'm sorry. I didn't mean to get upset."

"He's your friend. I know he means a lot to you, and I'm sorry he doesn't show you the respect you deserve. Now come on, why don't we get a take-out, huh? I'd love some Chinese."

"I love you, Tim."

"I know baby, and I love you."

JAKE
24 YEARS OLD

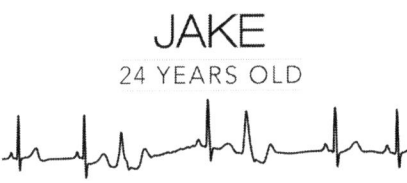

Fuck! I storm down the stairs and out of Lily's building. There is no fucking way I should feel like this. The blow I'd snorted off Yvonne's body should have kept me in check. Not to mention the amount of sex I've been having this week. She'd barely left my bed and happily supplied me with the white stuff.

Nothing has changed. I keep hoping that somehow this fucking pain in my chest, this incessant need to have Lily and claim her as mine will vanish. It never does. Every time I look into her eyes, I felt the rise of need within me. I want to steal her innocence and spoil it. Although I'm pretty sure she isn't quite as innocent as the sixteen-year-old Lily was, I want to bury my cock in her and see tears run down her face as I make her beg for me. I want to see her bent over ready for me. Those fucking dimples on her back had me grinding my teeth to stop from taking her in her fucking kitchen. One flash of creamy skin is all it took. She is everything I want. Her sexy, curvy figure had my cock hard in a flash.

But, she's moved on. She is living her life. She is happy. While my life was on pause because I can't fuck her out of my system. Nothing broke our connection. I worked my arse off at uni to prove to everyone I wasn't just a bad boy with a reputation. I kept the reputation and added success. But no matter what I did, how many girls I screwed, I am never satisfied.

Lily plays on the last remaining part of my soul that is pure, and I give in every time. She is my friend, but our friendship has fucked with my life for nearly ten years.

I am done.

God, I'm a bastard.

LILY
24 YEARS OLD

Hey, I don't know what happened the other night, but I hope we can still be friends. Lily

Jake? Are you there? Lily

I have to stop checking my phone. It's been three weeks and still nothing from Jake. I know deep down, that when he said good-bye, he meant it this time. I can't escape feeling so sad about it.

My shift ends in one more hour. One more hour until I can make it home and collapse into bed. I'm not sure if Tim has any plans for this weekend, but I know I'll be useless until I get a solid ten hours sleep.

"Tim, I'm home!" I pull my coat off and throw my keys into the bowl by the door. Warm light fills the hallway and front room. I take a few tentative steps into the house and see Tim waiting for me, leaning against the sofa. Candles cover the dining table, coffee table and any other surface I can see. The glow they emit is enough to light the whole room and my heart swells in my chest. He'd done this for me.

"Come on, sit, sit. I know you've been working really hard this week so I thought you deserved some pampering. I've put candles in the bathroom as well and as soon as you're ready, I'll run you a bath."

"Oh, Tim, this is wonderful." I practically collapse into his arms as he steps forward to meet me. I fit neatly against his chest, as if he was made especially to comfort me. Luckily, Tim wasn't shy in offering me all the affection I wanted or needed. He's always been happy to wrap me up in his strong arms. Tim seemed to know what I needed before I knew myself.

"It's my pleasure. If I can't spoil you and show you some love, who can?"

"Well, thank you. This week has been pretty gruelling and spending an hour soaking it all away sounds divine."

Tim plants a kiss on my temple and wraps me tighter against his chest. "Let's get you into that tub then. I don't want you falling asleep on the sofa." He takes my hand and leads me through to the bathroom where he's positioned more candles around the sink and bathroom cabinet. "Go and change and I'll get this sorted for you."

Half an hour later, I'm starting to prune in the warm water. I'm buried under a mountain of bubbles, but the soak has done the trick. I can feel the stress and tension drain from my limbs as if the water has dissolved the strain.

I pull myself through the bubbles and step out of the bath. I grab a towel, wrap it around me, and blow out the candles before going in search of Tim. There's no light from the living room but as I enter the bedroom I see a single candle lighting the room.

Tim's already in bed and lifts the covers in invitation as I enter. "Come on. It's late and we're both tired. We have the whole weekend to enjoy ourselves, but sleep now."

I drop the towel and dive into bed, seeking the warmth of Tim's body.

"Thank you." I wiggle against him so we fit together perfectly.

"Stop that, before I change my mind and ravage you instead." He pulls me tight against his body and plants a series of hurried kisses along my neck and I giggle and twist in his arms.

"This is just what I needed, baby. Thank you."

"It's my pleasure, Lily. It's my job to look out for the most important person in my life. Whatever I can. Even if it's just lighting a few candles to help you relax. Now, sleep." Tim pulls me in against his chest and I take a contented breath, utterly sated.

LILY
25 YEARS OLD

Hey, stranger. I'm in London on a hen party and thought we could catch up? You've not returned my texts, but you have my number. It would be nice to go for a drink. Lily

LILY
26 YEARS OLD

I don't know if this is still your number? I've not heard from you for a while, but I thought I'd try one last time.
Lily

That's it. No more text messages. No more reaching out. I don't even know why I still do it anymore. It's not like Jake's suddenly going to change his mind and answer me. I shouldn't even be thinking about Jake anymore. I put my phone on the bedside table and turn over. Tim was out this evening. A work party. Something to do with a big client they had won and that it was a compulsory evening. I'd grown used to a few late nights in his job. Last minute project briefs from the client or pitch presentations demanded the extra work. He had his sights on the creative director post and wanted to land it by the time he was thirty. I had every confidence he would.

My eyes drift closed and wonder if I'll still be awake when Tim arrives home.

Coffee. I'd really like a cup of coffee. My eyes are still closed and I fight against the weight in my limbs to turn over and wake up.

"Good morning." Tim smiles in greeting as my eyes focus on him. "I've made you coffee. Croissants are in the oven warming and then I need you up and out of bed."

"It's a Saturday."

"I know. But I have something special planned for us."

"Special?" I pull myself up to sitting and gladly take the mug of coffee from his hand.

"Yes. Today is just for the two of us. No friends, no work, no family. Just us, away from the city."

"Sounds perfect."

"That's the idea. Now, drink up and come and grab some breakfast."

I could have guessed where we are headed. It's a perfect autumn day. The sky is bright blue and free of clouds, but the sun can't take the chill from the air. Tim loves to take me to Westonbirt Arboretum. It's our slice of beautiful countryside right on our doorstep and today is a perfect day for it.

I bundle myself up with a hat and scarf and let Tim lead the way. We start off in the old arboretum. It's busy, with lots of families taking advantage of the sunny weather. The leaves on the trees have started to turn, and we're entertained by a rainbow of greens, golds and yellows.

"It's these days when we're not doing anything extraordinary and just enjoying each other's company that mean the most to me," Tim muses as we walk along, hand in hand.

"It is great to be able to get away and just enjoy a day to ourselves. You seem to know exactly when we need this. Thank you."

"If I had my way we'd be able to do things like this more often. I know we're both busy but I never want to lose sight of the small things. Being a family. Being there for each other." He pulls me in against him and wraps his arm around me. "I do love you, Lily."

My heart melts and I smile up at him. "I love you, too."

We continue our tour around the magnificent trees and enter the Silk Wood. The leaves are still crisp underfoot and I can't help but slide my feet through them to create the rustling, crunching sound like I did when I was a child.

The crowds have thinned in this part of the forest.

"This is all I'll ever need. You, happy, with me. We've beaten the odds Lil and made it. The only thing left is to put a ring on your finger."

"You're proposing!" The shock in my voice isn't subtle.

"Not today. But I want to marry you. I love you. You are all I'll ever want in life. I can't imagine being with anyone else and I want to make you my wife."

"Tim, that sounds awfully like a proposal."

"Take it as a promise. I need a ring first. So now would be the perfect opportunity to say if you're not ready to go along with this idea."

"No, no, I love the idea." My cheeks scrunch up as I smile so hard.

"Good."

"So we're not engaged?"

"No."

"But we will be?"

"Yes."

"Just so we're clear." Tim pulls me in and I lean my head against his shoulder. This has to be one the best days of my life. It's perfect.

JAKE
26 YEARS OLD

"Jake! Yes… More! Harder. Yeah, fuck me baby!" Yvonne shouts as I slam my cock into her wet pussy and fuck her as hard as I like. She always had a dirty mouth and I couldn't help but feel hard as nails for her when she started begging for more.

This is exactly what I need. I had to fuck the thoughts of Lily Hill out of my mind and if anyone can do it, Yvonne can.

I hook one of her legs over my shoulder and pump into her until I'm ready to shoot my load. *God, I fucking loved sex with Yvonne.* I grind into her and let her cries of pleasure spur me on. My back tenses as my own orgasm barrels through me. I collapse on top of Yvonne's sweat coated body and try to recover. "Umm, Jake. You never fail to be the best sex I've had."

"Well, don't get too used to it. I'm going back to London tomorrow."

"And I've told you I'd happily come and visit for a while. Last time I didn't get to see much of anything besides your bedroom."

"I think the reason we work so well Yvonne, is that we don't live in each other's pockets. Now, I've got to go. I'll give you a call next time I'm visiting." I roll off the bed and chuck the condom in the bin before pulling up my jeans. I finish getting dressed without a glance in Yvonne's direction and head towards the door. "See you soon."

If Yvonne kept asking about making our hook ups more permanent, I'd have to think about cutting her out of my life for good. She might be a great fuck and happy to fall into my bed anytime I snap my fingers, but she'll never be my girlfriend. No one will.

I head over to Andy's, after all, he's the reason I'm back in Bristol. It's his wedding tomorrow and there's no way I'll be able to get out of attending. I park the car and head up to his new house. I notice his own car parked outside the garage. It's the same fucking Audi S5 as mine. I grit my teeth together and pound my frustration out against the front door.

"About time, Jake. Where the fuck have you been?"

"Nice to see you too, brother." I don't wait for an invitation and head inside.

"Let me guess, you were too busy screwing Yvonne."

"Something like that." I turn around and look Andy in the eye. "What's it to you? You're getting married tomorrow. You shouldn't be concerned with who I spend my time with."

"Don't kid yourself, Jake. Yvonne is simply a plaything to me. I didn't realise she is still happy to fuck you."

"And I didn't realise you'd started cheating on Lisa." The tolerance I'd shown Andy when we were kids has been lacking for years. Now there is out and out hostility between us when we do meet up.

"If you can ever consider a real relationship, you might appreciate the position I'm in. What's good for you and what you want aren't always the same."

"No shit, Sherlock. Aren't we supposed to be toasting your happiness?" I've had about as much as I can take of Andy. I should be far more calm than I was, but his line about what I want and what is good for me just reminds me of who I don't have in my life anymore. Lily Hill.

No matter how much I try to forget her, I can't. It's like she's fucking etched into my soul. *God, I need a drink.*

9
LILY
31 YEARS OLD

I pull out the sheer black corset and cinch it around my waist and bust. The dress is already lying on the bed. I position it to make sure the corset doesn't show through, step into my heels, and grab my coat and purse before I head out. It's only a short walk to the club.

Aiden is working the door and doesn't hesitate to move the rope to let me through. I breeze past the check in desk and hand my coat to the cloakroom girl before scanning the room for my evening's entertainment.

My heels stick in the damp carpet as I head up to the top bar. The music blares, and its effect is immediate. The din quiets my mind and I relax. I rest my arms on the glass-topped bar and peer towards the bartender mixing a colourful cocktail. I grin and beckon him over. He's cute. And new. I wait for him to finish his order and am pleased he's taken note of my interest. He walks straight to me.

"Hi, what can I get you, beautiful?" He leans in to be heard over the music.

"Good evening. I'll have a glass of champagne, please."

"A lady with good taste."

"Yes. Very good taste," I purr in his ear.

He efficiently delivers my bubbles, but I'm in no hurry to rush off.

"What time do you finish your shift?" I lean in a little closer, and he takes advantage of the view of my boobs spilling out of my corset.

"Midnight. You want to wait for me?" He drags his eyes from my chest and brushes a lock of my hair to one side.

"As long as you don't mind me having a good time while I wait." It was a couple of hours until twelve, and I won't sit at the bar and wait. I do perch on a stool to finish my champagne.

The shadows hide the individuals on the dance floor, but I feel the energy that courses around the room. This is a place I can come and forget. I can leave real life at the door and do as I please. I've lived all of my life by the rules. Doing the right thing and working hard. Where was my magic pass? The world didn't reward kindness. It didn't protect love or life. Everything had been taken from me—my present and my future. So why should I care? Why should I play by the rules anymore? All I'd gotten was pain.

I tip my glass, drink the rest of the bubbles and place it back on the bar. I saunter through the crowd out to have a good time and nestle myself in the middle of the dance floor. The beat penetrates down to my bones, and I let my body relax into the music. A fog settles over my mind, and I feel myself drift away.

As the beats play on, the dance floor grows cramped with bodies and the touch and brush of flesh on flesh. A firm hand grips my waist, and pulls me back against his body. He encases me within his hold, and I reward his advance by pushing my backside against his crotch. He pulls me harder against him, and his cock digs into my bum.

I happily dance and grind with Mr. Anonymous as the hours tick by. My skin is clammy, and I'm in need of a drink, so I leave my dance partner to check on Mr. Barman. I approach the bar and take a seat on one of the empty stools. Most people are on the dance floor or secluded in one of the side booths. I look down the bar and see he's fixing a glass of champagne. He places the tall flute in front of me and accompanies it with a glass of clear liquid.

"Drink the water, enjoy the champagne. We can leave in about twenty minutes." I happily take his advice and enjoy the come down from the dancing. The water quenches my thirst, and the bubbles help to build the anticipation of what will come later.

I look out on the club floor and recognise a few regulars but make sure not to gain their attention.

"You looked like you were enjoying yourself. Ready for some more fun?" The deep, voice of the bartender pulls my attention. I turn towards him.

"I am. What did you have in mind?" I whisper in his ear, pulling the lobe between my lips.

"Hmm, keep that up, and we won't get far."

"Is that a problem for you?" I ask. He looks at me, and I see hunger and lust burn in his eyes. He grabs my hand and leads me from the floor. We head up another level and through a door marked 'staff only'. The corridor is dark and narrow, but we keep moving and head into an office of sorts. He shuts us in and the lock echoes around the small room.

He's on me in a second, hands tangled in my hair, lips desperately kissing me.

The hum that precedes the magical place where I simply don't care climbs my spine, and I welcome the feeling of letting my body get pulled about by Mr. Eager. He bites at my chest, sucking the skin to try and mark me as his other hand works up my thigh and under my thong.

"Oh yeah, you're fucking horny baby. You've made my fucking week." He fucks my pussy with his fingers, and I grind down to satisfy my own need. I want to get off as much as he does. "Lean back on the desk and pull your dress up."

I do as instructed, making sure my dress still covers my abdomen. He is too occupied with getting a look at what's between my legs to notice anything else, so I don't have to worry.

I open my legs wide and let him look his fill. He kneels down and pushes my knees wider. His tongue swipes through my wetness before thrusting deep and hard. His lips eat at my pussy, lapping at my core in fast strokes. Each brush of my clit stirs my release.

"Put a condom on and fuck me already," I pant.

"Yes, ma'am." He stands and unbuckles his belt to release his cock. I watch him slide the condom on before I jump off the desk and turn around to present him with my arse.

"Jesus woman," he curses as he lines his dick up and slams into my waiting core. His hand runs up my spine, and he yanks me back down on him by my shoulder. His other hand digs into the scars on my hip, but I push the pain aside. He thrusts a few times before he loses all control and begins to hammer into me. The slap of skin against skin fills the small room, and it sounds dirty. I don't care. My mind checks out, and I let myself enjoy the anonymous sex.

Mr. Eager is exactly that. There is no way *he's* going to get me off, so I lift one arm and find my clit. I rub the small bundle until a wave of pleasure rolls over me, and my pleasure builds once again.

"Shit, God, I'm going to fucking come!" he shouts as I feel my own climax tense and spiral out around my body.

"Yes, shit…Yes." He stills his pounding and pulls himself out of me. A convenient box of tissues sit on the desk, and I help myself. I right my underwear and dress before smiling at the bartender and heading for the door.

"Wait, where are you going?"

"Home."

"Can't I at least have your name? I'd like to see you again."

"You might do when I come back here. This was a one-time thing. Sorry, I thought that was obvious." I tilt my head to the side.

Did he really expect a quick hook-up for sex in the club office to turn into something more?

I unlock the door and head back the way we came. I pick up my coat and walk home. It's just after 1:00 a.m. when I walk in. I strip off and dump the clothes in the wash basket and delve under the shower. The heat envelopes me, and the steam cocoons me further. I wash and scrub before shutting off the water. I towel off and leave my hair to dry naturally. I climb under the covers and rest my eyes, hoping for a peaceful night's sleep.

JAKE
31 YEARS OLD

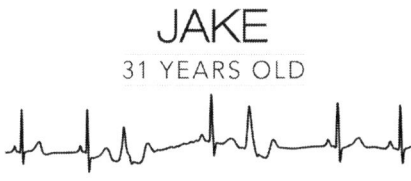

"*Where are you, Jake? I can't find you. I can't see…*"

"*I'm right here, can't you see me?*"

The girl's figure is just out of my reach. Her slender body is dressed only in a white slip dress decorated with flowers. The sky is a turbulent grey, threatening rain and storms.

"*I don't know where you are Jake. I need your help.*"

"*I'm here. I'm right here.*" *I can't move forward. I'm paralysed, frozen with no ability to move my legs or arms.*

"*You're not here. You're never here for me. You left me. You abandoned me.*"

The girl turns towards me, and I finally see her face. Lily looks at me. Her piercing eyes etched with pain and sorrow.

"Lily…" I bolt up in bed, sweat trickling down my torso.

"What is it, baby?"

"I'm not your baby." I check the clock. 2:00 a.m. "I think it's time for you to leave."

"Hey, we had a good time."

"Yeah, and time's up. You know where the door is." I toss back the covers and head for the bathroom. I turn the water on and wash the smell of drink, booze and sex from my skin—the usual cocktail to my weekends, and a lot of other nights as well.

I scrub away my evening of sin and go back out to the bedroom. I'm going to need a few more hours before I think about the office. As I open the door, the blonde is still sitting on the bed.

"I thought I told you to go. Leave now!"

"You really are a jerk."

"Didn't seem to think that when I was buried balls deep in your mouth last night. Leave, before I toss you out." I don't need this while my head is still pounding from my stupid fucking dream.

"You can't treat people this way!" She gets up as if she's going to stand her ground and make a point.

"Oh, and how do I treat them?" I prowl towards her and tower over her petite frame.

"Like this. You're tossing me out in the middle of the night."

"Did the quick fuck in the club before we even got here give you the wrong impression? I don't think so. Everyone knows my reputation. If you're so stupid you think you are going to be an exception, it's not my problem."

Tears sparkle in her eyes, and I curse myself for the enjoyment I get from seeing them there. "I said go!" I bellow. I watch as she scampers out of the bedroom and wait ten seconds before I hear the front door to my apartment slam shut.

I fall back onto the rumpled bed and close my eyes. The adrenaline has already started to flow, and I know it will be a while before I'm relaxed enough to sleep again. Still, keeping my eyes closed sure makes me feel like I am at least trying.

This fucking dream is starting to get old. Every few months it sneaks in and disturbs my sleep and leaves me feeling fucking awful for the next few days. Or until I can find some woman who doesn't mind my version of a one night stand.

I haven't been in touch with Yvonne in a couple of years. She had started to grow attached to our hook-ups—something I wasn't aware of until I fucked her friend at a party. In her warped mind, I was hers and no one was good enough blah, blah, blah. She started pulling some crazy stalker shit. That was never going to work with me and just made her look pathetic. Does it make me a fucking bastard that I missed the sex with her? I could do anything

I wanted, and she loved it. Always had. We'd built up a sort of trust over the years, but I wouldn't stand for her thinking she had a claim over me. No one has that. *Except for Lily.*

My eyes fly open at the thought of her again, and my mood sours further. What the fuck did I have to do to rid myself of my stupid fascination for this girl? I haven't spoken to her in five years, yet my conscience still thinks it can play games with me.

I jump out of bed, grab a pair of trainers and shorts and go to my home gym. I set up the treadmill and start a steady pace. Ever since I was a kid, I loved to run. It is a time to quiet my mind. Now I'm older, I enjoy the exercise, and it keeps my body looking good. I pummel the rubber tread with my feet and soon feel the natural high kick in as endorphins flood my system. Sweat coats my torso, but I push harder. When I work out at home, I have the advantage of collapsing right into bed when I finish. That's my aim now, single-minded exhaustion so I can sleep for a few more hours. Friday nights are usually spent at Harts, but the way I'm feeling now, I'm going to give it a miss.

Over the years, my behaviour hasn't improved. With age, a kick-ass job and the fact I know how good I am at what I do, both in the courtroom and the bedroom, I don't have to censor everything I say or do. Within reason. Clients don't want to see the bastard I am, not while I'm closing the deal.

Finally, my feet feel numb, and my lungs scream for more oxygen. I stop the machine and jump off, resting my hands on my thighs as I draw in a few deep, panting breaths. I kick off my trainers and fall right into bed. This time, the body sweat is entirely welcome and not the result of a girl who haunts my fucking dreams. I'm stronger than that. Lily won't rule my mind. No girl does that. *God, I'm a bastard.*

LILY

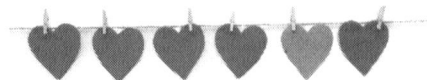

Friday is my favourite day of the week. It signals the end of the working week and the start of my quest to check out on life.

I'm not a physio any longer. I couldn't go back to my previous life and that included my old job. I didn't want to face the reality I was in. I didn't want the responsibilities of being a physio. I barely wanted to remember the life I used to strive for. Now, I am a receptionist. I can easily slide a mask over my pain and pretend to be a helpful and cheery person. Answering the phone, scheduling meetings, these things I can do mindlessly and they let me keep to myself. I don't work in a team or have people around me to start asking questions. It suits me perfectly. As soon as it hits 5:00 p.m., I take the mask off and go back to what my life has become. A constant quest to do as I want, without caring. There is nothing left for me to care about, so why bother.

I pull my favourite satin corset from the chest of draws and secure it around my waist and fit my boobs in. Firm boning and stitching enhance my cleavage and trim my waistline. It also makes me feel secure, as if the corset is physically holding me together. The tight fit also keeps my scars hidden. If I can ignore them, I don't remember the pain other than when the ache in my hip reminds me.

I didn't think you needed more than one little black dress until a few years ago. My signature outfit is efficient and a classic. Gone are all of the flowers, the innocent, sweet girl. She doesn't exist anymore. Black suits my mood and outlook, and I happen to look good wearing it.

Harts is my destination tonight. It has been a few weeks since I had visited the high-end club. It doesn't matter where I went, the goal and the outcome were almost always the same—drink, dance and do whatever I want.

The line of customers spilt out along the pavement outside of the dark building. I do my usual trick and go to see who is working the door. They all know me, and I'm confident I'll be let in like usual. Sure enough, the wall of bouncers parts and I'm let in. The whole ambience of Harts is designed to relax you, make sure you're having a fun time. Plush and luxurious furnishings line the entry way before you have to check in and pay the entrance fee. I'm pretty confident one of the top floors catered for private parties or private dancing, but that's not what I came here for.

Private booths line one wall of the main floor which is dominated by the dance floor. I strut past and head for the already crowded bar, filled with people not lucky enough or rich enough to be seated in the booths.

I nudge in between a few guys and wait to order my drink. I take the time to look up and down the bar to see who's out tonight. A young, preppy guy in a bow-tie looks like he's just won the lottery just being here. He's flanked by a tall man in a shirt who is trying his best to chat up the female bartender serving him. An older guy—or rather a similar age to me—waits patiently for his drinks to be delivered. His light suit and white shirt look good on him. His hair is neat and tidy, like the rest of him. I keep my gaze on him and hope to catch his eye.

"What can I get you, love?"

"A glass of champagne, please."

The cute guy looks my way as I wait for my drink and I offer him an inviting smile. I pay for my drink and slide away from the busy bar. Mr. Cute and Tidy crosses my path and gives me a cocky smile in return. He walks past me and heads to a corner of the club. I skirt the edge of the dance floor and watch the tangle of bodies as I sip my drink.

It's only a few minutes before the flute is empty and I head to mingle on the dance floor. I never enjoyed this in the past. I felt self-conscious and on display for everyone to see. Now, I don't have a conscience, and I want to be on display. As I wind my body through the swarming dance floor, my body begins to hum. The energy flows with every beat of the bass, and my mind clears of the stress and strain of the last few days.

The rhythm of the evening soon takes over; the smell of the sweat, the flashing lights that give you a snapshot of who's around you, the bass blocking out other noise as if you were in your own private party. They all wrap around me in a comforting blanket. The music blurs from song to song, and I get lost in the noise.

A tap on my shoulder brings me back earth. The guy with the cocky smile from the bar is holding a glass of champagne for me. I take it and drain it on the spot, handing it back to him before continuing to dance. He doesn't give up, which I give him points for, and returns to dance with me. It takes all of ten seconds before his hands are around my waist and pulling me closer to him. I go with it and continue to dance with him. He's lost the jacket and his white shirt flashes brightly under the lights. He's a good dancer and my arms wrap around his neck within minutes.

"I'm Nick."

"Lily," I reply. I shout in his ear to be heard.

"Pretty." He keeps up the close and personal, guiding the dance. I see him signal to someone behind me but keep dancing. A moment later I feel someone else push up against my back. Nick's face breaks into a smug grin. Perhaps he thought I'd baulk at the idea of two guys, but I no longer care what other people think. If it helped me to achieve the numb void where I can let my body experience pleasure without any strings, then I was game.

The two men must have worked this move before. They keep me pinned between them as they keep moving and swaying with the music. My arse is pressed up against the second guy. There is no way I can't rub into his crotch. My eyes stay fixed on guy one as we all continue to enjoy my lack of inhibitions. I drop my head back as I try and lose myself in the music again. Four hands cover my body, holding and moving my hips and waist. A hot flush creeps across my skin as the men work me this way and that, like a piece of meat between two hungry pups.

Guy one edges in closer, splitting my legs with his knee. He dips his head and forcefully takes my lips with his. It's hurried and harsh, but I don't push him away. He forces my body back up to guy two and I feel the hard plains of his body flush against my back. Guy one holds me in place so his friend can take what he wants. His fingers creep down my thighs, and my mind snaps awake for a second. One hand continues its journey and pushes up my skirt until he cups my arse cheek. He runs his finger between my legs and plays with the silken edge of my underwear.

With his other hand, he digs his fingers into my hair and pulls my head viciously away from guy one. He turns my face so he can take his kiss. Firm, purposeful lips play with mine in a sensual play as he coaxes my compliance. His tongue eases past my lips, and I have to halt the moan ready to erupt in my throat. *This guy can kiss!* It intoxicates me, and before I know what I'm doing, I've twisted so our bodies are pressed up against one another. I haven't seen this man's face or looked him in the eye, but I'm desperate for him to keep kissing me. Suddenly it's all I can think of. All I want.

JAKE

Nick has one thing on his mind tonight. He wants to be the lead and hook the girl first. It wasn't a big deal. He is as much a player as I am and doesn't give a shit what people think of him. Perhaps that's why we got on so well. He'd made his mark. Some brunette from the bar is already eyeing him up, so I'm biding my time. Sharing isn't my usual style, but it seems Nick wants a new challenge for tonight. Alcohol and attention can get you a long way towards doing whatever you want with a girl.

Nick has been on the dance floor for a while as I sit back and watch the show from the booth. His dance partner has a banging body, curves that beg to be held and long, tasselled hair that shakes down her back as she dances with Nick. She seems as eager as Nick is, no hesitation as to what she wants.

He finally signals for me to join the party and I happily cage the girl between us. To my surprise, she doesn't look around in shock or panic. She takes it in stride and keeps moving her hips in time to the music. The thought of screwing with her wakes my dick up, and I press in hard against her back. My hands are greedy to feel her body, and I wrap them around her hips and up to her waist. She drops her head back, clearly enjoying the attention. Nick's cocky grin hasn't left his face. He looks like he just hit the fucking jackpot with this girl and right now, with my dick pressed into her arse, I think he might be right. She's confident and sassy without throwing herself at us.

Nick pushes her closer against my body, trapping her tighter and goes to kiss her. My hands aren't satisfied with the feel of her dress. They run down the side of her until I reach the hem, and I slip one hand up her thigh. Firm, warm skin greets me, and I move them higher, pushing her dress out of my way. I trail my hand between her bum and slide a finger against the seam of her underwear. Fuck! I can feel the heat from her core, and it's like a torch to my lust. My other hand grabs a fistful of hair and pulls her away from Nick. I take my turn.

Her lips meld with mine, and she opens under my dominance. She tastes sweet and innocent which sends my mind spinning. I drown in that kiss, losing myself to it for a moment. The lust burns rampant and unchecked, and then she twists and pushes her body up against mine. *Holy fuck I want this girl.*

I break the kiss and release my grip on her hair. I look down at her face and stare as she opens her eyes. Deep pools of blue stare up at me, and I feel like I just stepped back in time. An ache radiates in my stomach from where I've just been punched. *Lily?*

No! This isn't happening. This can't be Lily. This isn't my Lily.

My Lily was pure and sweet and so innocent I'd never be able to imagine her acting this way. No, she wasn't like this. She wouldn't let two guys tag-team her on the dance floor of some club. She wore flowers, and her eyes made me see hope, if only for a second. As I look at her now, I take a step back, distancing myself from the blow she just landed. My mind churns with years of memories that all collide together and make the Lily in front of me out to be an imposter. I need to walk away. I can't do this with Lily.

The war in my chest threatens to break out of my ribs. All my past longings mix with the lust that boils in my veins. The kiss is embedded on my lips, and I'm utterly torn between what I want to do and what I should do. The throb of my cock didn't help the situation. I can't. I need to walk away. Lily still has power over me. She'd turned from a dream into a nightmare. Five, six, seven years, whatever the distance between us, I can't let her in and don't need to hate myself for finally giving in and fucking her.

I look back at her, ready to leave with my conscience intact, but she smiles, licks her lips and lifts her delicately shaped eyebrow in challenge.

Everything changes at that moment. I forget she was my friend. I forget the guilt that used to claw through me when I thought about being with her. I'd grown up and had a much more literal appreciation of what I could do to her now, and it only fuelled my imagination further. Every woman I'd been with has been a substitute for this girl in some way or another. And here she is, looking like my every fucking fantasy, just waiting for me. We weren't in school anymore. We were both adults. What was stopping me? She is only a few feet away, so I close the distance and loom over her. She looks like the cat who got all the fucking cream. That is my green light. I'd never seen her like this but right now, Lily was begging for me to see this through. *God, I'm a bastard.*

10
LILY

Jake? Recognition strikes. I look through the patchy light and see my friend. He still possesses the bad boy demeanour that earned him his reputation. He looks stronger, more muscled and chiselled than when I last saw him. *No.* I push the thought aside and focus on the here and now.

I just kissed Jake Stewart. A whisper of an old self struggles up from within me. I remember how much I longed for Jake, how I hoped he would always notice me. He finally had, and I can still feel the sensation tingling on my lips. Heat and desire surge through me and I see the opportunity to have something I always wanted. Why shouldn't I? As our eyes lock again, I decide to make it obvious. He's as stunned as I am, but I don't want to give him the time or the space to dismiss this. My tongue brushes over my full bottom lip in invitation and I arch my brow, challenging him. We're not sixteen anymore and right now, I want to find out what being with Jake is all about. In fact, I need it.

"Got to say it, I didn't expect the Jake Stewart I knew to back away from a girl in a bar."

"Who says I'm backing away?"

His jaw firms at my challenge.

"Well, then why are we still talking?"

"You need to be careful, Lily."

"Why? Give me one good reason."

Nick seems oblivious to what's going on between me and Jake, and feels it's time to put himself back in the picture. His body presses up against mine and I freeze, like a solid rod of metal has been thrust into my spine. He tries to encourage me to dance, but I don't want to. Jake is standing in front of me.

As soon as Nick's hands circle and begin to grope over my stomach and chest, I see Jake's nostrils flair before his eyes train in on Nick. He removes his hands and levels Nick with a stare that would intimidate anyone.

"Back off, Nick. Change of plans," he yells over the roar of the music. Nick stops his hands but doesn't let me go.

"I don't think that's your decision to make, Jake."

"Fuck off!" He stabs his finger at Nick and fixes his eyes on me. He's far from pleased with the situation, but for some reason, that pleases me.

"What's wrong Jake? Don't want to share anymore?"

He snatches my arm and pulls me from Nick's grasp. He doesn't stop and drags me from the dance floor and towards the exit.

"In a hurry, are we?" I ask as we hit the frigid night air.

"Not particularly." He doesn't look at me, just keeps his steel grasp on my wrist. A taxi pulls up to the kerb, and he opens the door and ushers me inside. Jake reels off an address and sits back. He turns his face to the window, and I'm left wondering what the hell all of that was about. I let Jake take the lead for a moment. I got carried away, but I can't get wrapped up in a long-ago-forgotten fairy tale. My intentions for the night haven't changed. Just because this is Jake, it shouldn't affect me. It shouldn't. I've been the good girl, always played by the rules and it left me nothing but scars.

The quiet is suddenly too loud, and I need to keep the adrenaline coursing through my system. I slide my body closer to Jake and run a hand up his arm. I lean in until I can smell him and let his scent surround me. It's familiar, clean, and is somehow completely Jake. My lips plant a kiss against his neck as I breathe him in deeper.

Jake's head whips around, and he stares daggers at my advance. "Don't," he scolds.

"What is it, cold feet?" I pout at him.

"No, but if you don't stop that, I'm going to fuck you in the taxi, and I won't give a shit at what you say in protest. Got it?"

Silence descends after his little outburst, and I heed his warning. The taxi ride is short, and as we pull up, Jake throws the driver a twenty and pulls me out of the cab. We walk into the entry room and up to the second floor. He doesn't loosen his grip, doesn't check I'm alright, but pulls me along with intent and purpose. Each stride forward my heart beats harder, and my body comes alive.

When I think about the situation logically, it's ridiculous. A guy I used to know has dragged me out of a club and to his house, has barely said two words to me, yet I'm dizzy with anticipation. This is as against the rules as I can get, and my conscience hasn't put up any objection.

Jake tugs me into his apartment and lets the door shut behind us. The click of the door rings around the room. Jake takes my hair and grips it viciously, pulling it back as his other hand grips my jaw and he backs me up against the wall. He looks over my body, my skin spiking with goose bumps as his eyes trail over it. He's sizing me up like I'm a feast all for him, he just isn't sure what to taste first.

"Do you know how long I've thought about this? How long I've wanted to taste you, to touch you?" He slides his fingers from my jaw, and they trace down my neck, my chest and between my breasts. He's so close. His face is right up against mine, so close we share the same air. I breathe him in, and his smell keeps my pulse from skyrocketing.

His words seep deep inside of my soul, but I fight them. If I let them mean something, I'm going to fall into a pit of despair. I've avoided that for years. Jake can't break me just because he's muttered a few words to me. I am stronger than that.

"Why don't you start showing me some of your bad boy reputation instead of just posturing, huh?" I lick the side of his mouth and cheek, hoping it will stir him to action. I don't want to be reminded of who I used to be. There is too much pain to wade through first, and I buried it for a reason. I'm just fine with who I am now.

Jake's growl reverberates in his chest, and it charges the air between us. He strikes my neck first, biting his teeth into my sensitive skin. It's as if he short-circuits my ability to bear weight on my legs. I feel weak next to him, and a moan pulls free from my throat. Liquid heat erupts and pools between my thighs. His lips travel over and around my neck, nipping and biting harder and harder.

Finally, he slams his lips into mine. The bruising pressure lights up my mind and my hands climb around Jake's neck. The cold, hard wall presses against my back, and I have nowhere to hide, so I don't. I take everything he gives me. His dominance and aggression are present in every muscle of his body. I feel the tension in his arms as I run my greedy hands over him. He allows my hands to wander unchecked, and I explore as I pull him closer against me.

He grinds his pelvis into me, and I feel his thick erection press against my abdomen. It sets my lust burning, and I take a step closer to that beautiful place where my mind lets my body take over.

Jake moves his hand and slides it between us, fumbling with

his belt. His lips leave mine, and I gasp for air as we part. The clang of the buckle and his zip tell me what he's doing. He takes a step back, distancing his warmth and with his other hand, he presses on my shoulder forcing me down. There's no room to miss his intentions.

I kneel in front of him and stare up at him. His eyes are hooded, and the hazel colour has been taken over by the dark of his pupils. He looks every inch the bad boy, and I press my thighs together at the thought of tonight.

His hand strokes his cock, sliding over the smooth skin. "Open." He commands.

I part my lips, and he presses the head into my mouth. The salty tang hits and saliva pools in my mouth. Before he pushes to the back of my mouth, he withdraws and shoves hard and fast back in, pushing his cock deep down my throat. I fight the urge to gag and try and breathe through it. Jake's hands come down to press my head tight against him, leaving me no option than to take what he's giving me. Each stroke chokes my throat and my eyes burn as tears pool. Saliva is forced from the corners of my lips as I stretch around his width, trying to accommodate him. Drool trails down my chin, and I try to relax against his intrusion.

Jake tilts my head back with a yank of my head and stares down at my tear stained face. He smiles as he lets out a groan and then rams back into my mouth. The burn of my tears spreads to my chest as I struggle to breathe, pulling air through my nose and trying to time my breaths with his pumps. It's degrading and dirty, and he shows no care for me as he takes his pleasure, but I don't care. This isn't about pleasure for me. It never is. It's easy to be used and to be able to lose myself for a few moments. I can do this.

He ploughs deeper inside my mouth and holds his cock deep in the back of my throat before pulling out. A trail of saliva clings to his cock as he withdraws. He grabs and pulls me from my kneeling position, and we're back to him dragging me about. The house whizzes past me as we head to the bedroom. He spins me around to him and our lips collide. Our bodies slam into each other. Jake scrambles to push my dress from my body. I help him with the zip and let him reveal my corset underneath. He takes a second to run his eyes over my satin covered form. "Fuck, Lily."

The moan stirs something in my chest. I ignore the twinge and the longing in his voice and get to work on undressing him.

As his clothes hit the floor, I get my chance to view his sculpted chest. A raging heat eclipses me the moment I touch his smooth skin. We both dive into a frenzied grapple of hands seeking skin, trying to get closer to each other. Jake's height gives him the advantage, and he uses it to overpower me, moving me toward the bed. He shoves me down and removes his boxers before climbing over me. His eyes are still void of colour and look deadly. I shrink on the inside as I think about what he could do to me, but his lips against my ankle block the thought. It's such a tender gesture it stuns me. It doesn't last long as his fingers reach for my hips, and he yanks the elastic, pulling my underwear off. He takes another pause, and my temperature soars under his scrutiny. He kneels up over me and pulls me closer to him with my legs.

"Condom," I pant. He drops my legs and opens a drawer on the table next to the bed. He's back and rolling protection on his thick shaft. He hoists my legs up, and I wrap them around his waist. He holds his cock and rubs the tip through my wet folds before he surges forward and slams into me. I arch and groan at the forceful intrusion. Jake doesn't give me a second to adjust and sets a punishing rhythm, thrusting in hard and sharp. My body wants to protest, and I can feel my muscles tense up, but I fight to stay relaxed.

"I want to see your tits. Play with those perfect tits for me, Lily." Desire strangles his words and he growls between breaths.

I'm not taking the corset off, but I do want to show him what he's asked for. I unfasten the first two hooks and shift the corset down to display my breasts.

I roll the soft flesh in my hands, pushing and squeezing them between my palms. Jake's hungry eyes are transfixed and consume every movement of my hands. He drops my thighs and leans down to suck a nipple into his mouth. The warmth dissolves the edge of pain he was punishing me with. His tongue swirls and his teeth bite, and my body gives in to him. He runs his free hand up the outside of my hip and waist while he continues to lavish attention on my chest.

His fingers wrap around my neck. The pressure is enough to make me panic for a moment. He bites down on my breast and squeezes my throat as he thrusts inside of me. Every muscle in my body tenses and I hear the rush of blood. My heart echoes inside of my head. My arms move up around his shoulders as he breaks his hold and I gasp and cling to him, trying to anchor myself to something as my brain clicks back on.

The empty void I seek is filled with Jake. My heart stampedes; my body sweats, and despite my head telling me this is wrong, my body relaxes under him.

"You feel so fucking good, Lily."

He feels good, too.

My thighs are slick, and our bodies slide across each other effortlessly.

I dig my nails in and score his back as I try to bring him closer to me. His head arches back, and he groans, a visceral, sexy sound and turns my body into a desperate mess of desire. My nails dig in harder, and I run my hands up to his hair, pulling him down to my lips. I start to move under his thrusts, pushing up to meet him and grinding down onto him. My teeth bite at his lips, and I plunge my tongue deep into his mouth. My mewls of desire stream from my mouth as my desire builds in the pit of my stomach.

"Fuck!" Jake leans up over me again, his hand presses against my lips, stopping me from crying out in pleasure. Sweat dampens the hair around his temples, and his muscles form beautiful contours over his tense body. He fucks me wildly, chasing both of our climaxes.

My legs strain and I feel the coil in my stomach. I drop my legs from his waist and open myself to him as much as physically possible.

"Fuck, yes, yes!" he cries as his eyes stare at me.

I'm so close, my eyes plead with him to push a little bit further to release my own storm of pleasure. My cries sound against his hand as he continues to try and silence me. Finally, the wave crests and I come hard as he slams inside of me. All of my muscles spasm and contract and my back arches involuntarily. Our connection breaks as my eyes close and my head rolls to the side.

Jake's hand slips from my lips, now numb from the pressure, and I take a deep breath. He falls to the side, flopping onto his back. Neither of us say anything. I turn to my side and keep my eyes closed as I try and settle my racing heart. I wanted the oblivion that living my promiscuous life had given me. But as I lie here my head whirs with thoughts of Jake. This is Jake. I just had hot, awesome, dirty sex with Jake.

I bite my lip and scrunch my eyes. So what if this is Jake. It's still just a hook up. I shouldn't treat it any differently to the countless others times over the last few years. I wasn't after a relationship. I did whatever I chose and didn't care for the consequences. This was an exception. *An unbelievably amazing exception.*

Moments slip past in silence, not even the rustle of the bed covers reach my ears. I hold my breath and turnover and risk a glimpse at Jake. His eyes are closed, and his face is calm. Gone are the lines of strain he carried earlier. Seeing him like this, I can't help but remember him as the teenager I gladly gave my heart to. I lower my lips and plant a kiss on his forehead before I slip out of bed. I put myself back together and tip-toe out of the room and exit the apartment.

JAKE

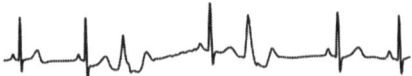

*L*ight creeps into my mind and disturbs my slumber. Morning.

God, I hadn't crashed like that after sex in forever. *Lily.* I turn to my side with a grin on my face, but it turns to a scowl in record time when I see the empty bed. "Lily?" I shout as I drag my body out of bed. The dress I peeled her out of, her shoes and bag, are all gone. "Fuck!" Rage fills me as I storm to the kitchen and look around the apartment. No sign of her, no note, no number.

Doubt quickly mixes with the anger that burns through my blood. I can't remember speaking to her before I passed out. Shit, satisfying sex is one thing, mind blowing, fucking fantastic sex was another. I'd screwed around enough to know the difference, and I never thought I'd get that with Lily. I had always assumed her innocent, sweet nature extended to the bedroom. But after the dirty, unrestrained fucking that had just taken place, I couldn't have been more wrong—or more delighted than I was. I head to the bathroom and pull the light switch. I twist and stare at the vivid red claw marks etched into my back. Last night definitely did happen. Lily Hill let me deep throat her, fuck her senseless and smother and choke her. *What the fuck?* Why wasn't I feeling better about this?

Fifteen years of wanting had given me a lot to think about when it came to Lily. She was fucking perfect last night. She didn't back down; didn't tell me to stop or take it easy. The dirty, raunchy sex was everything I get off on when I'm with some random girl. The Lily I used to know would have fled in horror. That was the whole fucking point of staying away from her. What the fuck happened to turn her into such a different woman? When did the Lily of my childhood disappear?

A feeling I'm not familiar with twists in my gut. Guilt.

I take a scalding shower and try to shake the unease that has wrapped me. It's unnerving. I never feel guilty about fucking a woman. Ever. Can I really put Lily in the same box as the other women who've drifted in and out of my life?

I dry off and sit on the edge of my bed as I reach for my phone and search for her number. I never deleted it. Despite cutting all contact, I couldn't just erase her. I fire off a quick message.

Sorry I missed you this morning. How about we catch up?
Jake

Lily is doing exactly what I would do after hooking up on a night off. She's completely turned the tables on me, and I fucking hate it. I feel powerless when all I really want to do is have a conversation with her. After all this time, she thinks she can waltz back and screw around and disappear again? No fucking way.

11
LILY

Two weeks later

Seeing Jake has rocked me. It has been two weeks, and I can finally admit it to myself. The little blip I felt from my heart after sleeping with him hasn't made another appearance since that night, but I couldn't get past the fright it gave me.

The last few years I've been living my life on autopilot. I don't care about anything and if I don't care, I can't get hurt or feel pain. Everything I did was to avoid feeling and to keep my memories buried. Jake is a huge risk to disturbing my carefully constructed world. I can remember being the girl who thought he was larger than life, the most handsome, intriguing boy I'd met. But I can't separate those thoughts from the rest of my memories I'd locked in a box. Tim, the accident, the pain. It was all under lock and key, and I won't let Jake break it open.

Running away was what I always did now. Have some fun, clear my head and pretend I'm someone else, get out.

Seeing Jake's name flash up the morning after wasn't what I expected. His past reputation certainly wasn't for a repeat performance. Or any further contact for that matter. I don't reply and push the detailed memory of his body working with mine into another box I mentally mark with a 'do not enter' sign.

I ignore the further two messages he sent later that week. It was the safest option for my future sanity. I knew my behaviour was self-destructive enough without any help from Jake.

I'd kept a low profile for the first week after seeing him. I stayed home and tried to forget. If I went out, I didn't want to risk meeting him again. Especially if he is trying to get in contact. Luckily, Shoreditch offered plenty of places to forget my concerns and get back to my usual routine.

There are more appointments at work than usual this week, and there is a group of gentlemen who have been in meetings for the last few days. One of the suits has been especially blatant with his visual appreciation of my cleavage. He's cute and quite sexy, and I happen to overhear their plans for tonight. They are staying in the city for the weekend and are planning to go out to XO tonight. It seems like a pretty good idea to me.

I book a taxi for the short ride to the club. The heavens have opened, and the rain pelts the concrete floor. No way I am walking anywhere in the deluge tonight. The taxi delivers me right to the door and luckily, there is no line. I check my jacket and enter the main club room. I've been to the clubs enough to know their individuality. I'm sure it would appeal to other women, but I just want to get to the main event. I hear the music, I enjoy the alcohol, and I get lost in the freedom to act however I chose. The clubs provide an anonymity I like.

The bar is my first stop, and I order my usual. It's not long before I spot the group who have been at work. They're taking up a large table and sofa area that's cornered off. I position myself so I'm clearly in view and wait until I spot the cute guy.

"Hello." A whisky smooth voice whispers in my ear. I turn to see the man I was searching for.

"Hi. Fancy running into you here." I smile and do my best impression of looking coy.

"A happy coincidence. Join me?" He offers his arm, and I

accept as he leads me across to join his friends. He pulls me down into his lap as he takes his seat on one of the sofas. This guy clearly doesn't have any issues with being forward and that works just fine with me. He strokes my arm as he surveys the conversation going on around him. I sip my champagne but the music calls me. I want to dance.

"So how long is appropriate to sit here with you before I can excuse us and fuck you?" Mr. Presumptuous whispers. I hold in my spurt of laughter.

"Well, I think you're getting ahead of yourself. You've not even bought me a drink." I shake my almost empty glass at him. "And you haven't danced with me yet."

"I'm sure I can accommodate your wishes. As long as I get to wrap your legs around me later, I'm sure you can get me to agree to anything."

His line makes me cringe, and a sliver of regret enters my mind about coming here. I stand and head to the dance floor, but he grabs my hand to steer me to the bar first. His arm coils around my waist and trails over my bum.

I've dealt with my fair share of pricks, it comes with being outwardly promiscuous, but this guy is creepy. He buys me a glass of bubbles, and I lead the way to the dance floor. He's over me like a rash before I can even start to move. This is not what I want when I come out. I make sure I have fun with the guys I flirt with. His hands are all over my body, and it turns my stomach. I beat them away and turn out of his grasp, but he doesn't get the message.

JAKE

XO is a little closer to the city than I usually venture, but I've had no luck bumping into Lily again. She'd put me in a complete funk. Every time I hooked up with a girl, all I saw was Lily's face as I made her come. She had effectively killed any interest I had in other women.

I enter the club room and scan the bar and dance area. It's still early, and so it's not too busy. I make my way to the bar and grab a bottle of beer and watch the dance floor. A few minutes later I catch a glimpse of a silhouette that has me moving across the bar. It's Lily. *Finally.*

My satisfaction is short lived as I watch her being manhandled on the floor by some jerk. Watching her twist and turn makes me see red. A possessive rage hijacks my senses and my body moves to put a stop to this guy. I don't want Lily to be in anyone else's hands except for mine. My arms reach to pull the jerk off her, and I push him to the side. I feel pretty fucking good about myself for stepping in, but Lily gives me a look that has me second guessing my actions. Her brows knit together in her version of a scowl. She's pissed. She slams her palms against my chest.

"What do you think you're doing?"

I grab her arm and pull her against me. "Looking after you. It was pretty fucking obvious you couldn't handle yourself with that guy."

A hand grabs my shoulder and pulls me back. The jerk is attempting to intimidate me and failing. I don't fucking care. He's not going to touch Lily again.

"Hey, man. Mind your own fucking business. The lady is with me."

"I don't think so." I still have Lily's arm clenched in my grip, and I pull her away from the dance floor.

"Jake, what the fuck!" she screams at me, but I don't take any notice. "Jake, stop. You can't do this."

"Wanna bet?" I turn to her and stare her down.

"One night doesn't mean you own me."

"No? Well tough. You didn't look like you were enjoying his hands all over your fucking body, so let's just consider I did you a favour, huh?"

"Let go of me."

She continues to struggle as I exit the club room and turn her toward the cloak room. "Did you have a coat?"

She gives me a dramatic huff and rolls her eyes at me. It helps to settle the completely undefined behaviour I'm currently exhibiting but doesn't go far enough for me to loosen my grip on her. She digs out a ticket from her bra and hands it over.

We collect her things, and I release her for a moment to help her with her coat. Next, I march us outside.

"Where do you think we're going, Jake? You've made your point. Now let me go."

"Not a chance. You're coming back to mine."

"I don't think so. That was a one-time thing."

The rain hasn't let up, and it drenches us as we snap at each other. My wet clothes don't come close to dampening the fire that's raging inside of me for this girl. My mind has hit a one-way track that involves getting Lily back to my place so I can explain a few things to her.

Her hair darkens as the rain soaks her through to her skin. She's too angry to notice, and now, all I want to do is kiss her. So I do.

I slam my lips against hers. Her body stiffens, but as soon as I part my lips and let my tongue stroke her bottom lip, her arms wrap around my neck, and she gives in. She moves her mouth over mine, and we both grow greedy. Heavy raindrops run down our faces and seep between our lips.

"I'm taking you home, and I don't want a fucking argument." I moan into her mouth, desperate to keep the contact with her.

I pull my eyes away and look for a taxi.. We're in luck. One waits nearby. I grab her hand and lace our fingers together and pull her in the direction of the waiting car. We're both panting as we dash through the rain and jump in. The journey is quiet and so is Lily's body language. She doesn't make any attempt to get close or continue the kiss that made me feel like a teenager again.

The quiet journey is what I need to get hold of my scrambled thoughts. Fuck! Seeing Lily with some other guy lit me up with jealousy and anger, but I don't do emotions over women. I boil with resentment. This is her fault. Her and her stupid out of character behaviour.

We arrive home, and I pay the driver and usher Lily into my building. Unlike her previous visit, I don't have only sex on my mind. I open my apartment door and let her in. I turn and double lock the door with the key before following her into the kitchen. There is no way she is sneaking out without talking to me in the morning.

"Would you like a drink? Or a towel, perhaps." I've already stripped her body of every shred of her soaked clothes in my head. But I need to slow things down. For now.

"Do you have champagne in your fridge?" she asks in such a way I can't miss the challenge.

"No, I only have champagne when I'm celebrating. I don't think we're celebrating tonight." I walk to the fridge and pull out two bottles of beer and leave one on the breakfast bar for her. She walks cautiously across and picks it up, wearily, as if it could hurt her. She puts it back down and leans on the bar facing me.

"Why, Jake? Judging by your behaviour before you realised it was me the other week, your reputation and behaviour haven't changed. Why did you have to interfere?"

"And you wanted that sleaze ball all over you? And don't you fucking dare lie. I saw you pushing him away. You were practically having sex on the dance floor with Nick and me without a care in the world. This was different. You didn't want this guy all over you, and I was there to help."

"And who said you could swoop into the rescue? I'm a big girl and can look after myself." Her cheeks grow pink as she gets louder and more cross. All it does is short my brain and make me think of making her whole body flush as I fuck her again.

"I wanted to rescue you. I didn't want his hands on you." I take a few steps towards her until I'm standing over her and staring down into her beautiful eyes. They hold a mix of confusion and lust and right now, I want the lust to win out. I watch as the stormy blue grows dark as her pupils dilate. My smile ticks at the corner of my mouth before I plunder her lips. I take my time, caressing and rolling my mouth against hers.

This evening I'm determined not to hurry things. Last time I was so revved up I fucked her with a blind focus. Tonight, I want to take my time with her. Play out my fantasies with her. She'd already ticked all the boxes for me. She could handle me when I was harsh and when I was cold. I didn't need to worry about hiding behind the mask I used to wear for her.

"I think you're angry, Lily, and that's going to make for some seriously hot sex. But I won't fight you all the way. Admit the guy was a jerk and you are glad I snatched you out of there."

She bites down on my bottom lip which makes my dick throb with need. I force my eyes to stay on hers. I see mischief and sex shining back, and it pumps my blood faster to my dick. She releases me, stepping back and picking up her beer.

"I'm only glad because I know how good you are in bed. I don't need you, Jake."

Her taunts fire my aggression and my hands ball into fists at my side. She tips the beer into her mouth, and I watch as she takes several long pulls. I've never wanted to fuck her, or anyone else, as much as I do right now. I want to mark her skin and look into her soul as I make her come and scream my name.

If she wants to play games, so be it. I'll play with her, but it will be by my rules. I'm practically salivating with thoughts of her body ready for the taking.

"Take off the dress." She cocks her head to the side and shakes it. "Take off the dress, Lily." She still doesn't comply and hops up onto the breakfast bar.

I abandon the last grip on my patience and storm across the few feet that separate us. I bend and all but throw her over my shoulder and carry her into my bedroom. All I need is a club to drag along the floor, and the Neanderthal analogy is complete.

I toss her on the bed and flip her onto her stomach. My legs straddle her backside and imprison her as I find the stupid zip and set about removing her dress.

"Get off of me!" she shrieks.

Her bucks and wiggles only serve to excite me further. I pull the dress down and find another layer blocking my path to her beautiful skin. We both fight against the dress coming off, but I win and pin her back to the bed with my weight covering her.

"Now, shall we see if you're really objecting to this, hmm?" My hand moves between her thighs and snatches her barely-there thong out of the way. Slick, warm heat greets my fingers as I run them through her pussy. Her moan makes my dick kick against my jeans.

"Oh, baby. You're enjoying this. Your body tells me you're liking everything I'm doing to you." I push two fingers deep inside her and watch her body relax.

"You're a fucking bastard, Jake."

I chuckle to myself. "Really? Am I bastard when I do this?" I curl my finger up inside her and run the pad of my finger across the rough spot that will drive her crazy.

"Hmmm," she moans into the bed, trying to stifle her cry. A flood of juice coats my fingers as she spreads her legs in welcome.

"See, you're desperate for me to fuck you again. Can't wait to spread your legs for me." She thrashes and her hands screw up the covers in her frustration.

"You know, I don't understand why you didn't just get this over with all those years ago," she moans. *What the fuck!* My free hand holds her back while I pull my fingers away. I hear the whine she makes and smirk to myself. Without any warning, my palm smacks down onto her peachy arse. The shock radiates through her body, and I watch in delight as she squirms.

"That hurt." Her complaint falls on deaf ears, as I smack her again. "Oww!"

I release her and flip her onto her back. Her corset makes me want to drool all over her. She looks so sexy, but right now I want it off. With hurried fingers, I set about springing each of the hooks open to reveal her milky white skin.

"Stop it. Leave it on."

"Not a chance." I wrestle her arms back above her head. I'm getting tired of her feigned attempts at fighting. I tear the thick, black material from her body and gaze at her like a starving man at a feast.

First, I want to give her another taste of what I like.

"Don't move." I point at her and move across to the wardrobe. I pull out two ties and return.

"Hands together, out in front." She sits up and complies with a smile. She's got no trouble with what I want to do to her. I wrap the material and secure her wrists with one of the ties.

"I only want to hear how much you enjoy me fucking you. No more talking." She can't hide the slight look of confusion on her face before I push the tie between her lips, gagging her and tying it in place. She looks like every fucking fantasy I've ever had of her. I push her back down and raise her arms above her head so I have uninterrupted access to every inch of her.

My hungry mouth descends, and I lick my way from one nipple to the other. I swirl the tip and bite down until she arches against me. I lick, suck and bite over her chest and breasts until her skin blushes, and her sighs and moans grow loud behind her gag.

I strip my clothes and grab a condom from my table.

"On your knees." I twist her onto her front and viciously tug her hips up. My fingers knead her plush arse, but I'm too impatient. I grab the base of my dick and push at her entrance, slamming into her as hard as I can. Her tight pussy strangles my dick, and I hear the unmistakable cry from behind my tie. I pull out and drive in again, taking her hard. I yank her hips backwards as I thrust forward and fuck her with abandon.

The feeling eats me up, and I feel cum threatening to burst out of my eager cock. I pump a few more times, drawing out each stroke to the maximum before slipping out of her completely. Every nerve of my body screams in complaint, but I don't want to come like this. I want to watch her eyes as I make her come.

I manhandle her onto her back, her hair spilling over the pillow as I move her to the right position. She automatically lifts her arms above her head and feels for the posts of the headboard.

"Good girl."

I split her legs and hook them around my hips and drive back into her hot sex. Her eyes flutter shut and her moans hum in the air.

I rock a few times, making sure I hit her clit as I do. Every time I do, she whimpers. Her sounds affect me like a hit of speed. I ram into her harder, seeking those beautiful, stifled cries. She turns her head and hides her face. It pisses me off, so I grab her chin and force her to look at me.

"Open your eyes, Lily." She jerks her head away and buries it next to her outstretched arm.

"Look at me!" I shout. Her defiance frustrates me beyond reason. I don't want this to be an anonymous fuck. I want to see her. I want to watch as her pupils blow as desire overtakes her.

"Fuck!" I curse loudly as rage and my release climb my spine. I hitch her leg higher, hooking it over my shoulder so I can go as deep as I can and pump into her. She keeps as hidden as possible, but her moans escape louder and louder.

"Don't do this, Lily. Don't hide from me when I'm fucking you." I give her one more warning. Hell, I don't think I can contain the need that's tearing through me with every move I make.

I quicken my pace and attune myself to each reaction I draw from Lily. Her breathing is rapid, and sweat coats her brow. Her tits jolt with each thrust of my cock and mesmerise me.

Her pussy weeps with her juices and I fight back my impending climax. I want her to come. I kneel, and let her leg slide from my shoulder. My hand zeros in on her clit and I press down hard. The muscles in her body all contract at once and she squeezes my cock, sending blinding flashes of pleasure to my brain. I do it again and listen to the whimpers that would fill the room as screams if she wasn't gagged.

I assault her with both my hand and my cock and watch her chest heave as her orgasm hits and she convulses around me. I hammer into her, chasing my climax now I've given her hers. She relaxes under me, and I feel her sated bliss radiate through me. I run my hands up the centre of her torso and squeeze her nipple.

She milks my cock as I come hard, grunting loudly in relief as my orgasm barrels up and explodes through my body. *Fuck me!*

I tug the gag from her mouth and watch as she wets her lips. She manoeuvres her wrists and sets a hand free before she drops them to the side and just lies there, exhausted, sucking in air. This isn't Lily. This isn't the Lily I remember, anyway. There's no denying she's getting off on the sex. She couldn't possibly fake her body's reactions. But she's not in this with me. Her eyes don't focus. The innocent girl I swore to myself I'd stay away from is not the same girl lying stripped and exhausted beneath me. I watch as her chest rises and falls. My eyes drink her in, and I notice two red scars across her lower stomach and hip. My hand reaches out to rub them.

"Don't." She grabs my hand and stops me. It's the only word she's said to me, and it pisses me off. She pushes me off her, climbs out of bed and heads to the bathroom before I can ask her about them.

I should be utterly satisfied after sex, but I wanted more. I didn't want her to brush me off and put this down to another easy fuck.

At least, this time, she's not going to be able to sneak out on me. We didn't talk last time, but she isn't leaving until we get things straight. Right now, that means giving me her number and promising she won't screw anyone except me. No way am I going to let Lily go. *God, I was a bastard.*

12
LILY

I will not cry. I will not cry. I turn the tap on and splash water over my face. Being here is a mistake. A fucking huge one. There is no way in the world I am strong enough to keep my vacant appreciation of life going with Jake in it. He's too much. Too familiar, too handsome, too good. I'm already starting to remember, remember what it felt like to be sixteen. To worry about school and boys and exams and think they were the most important things in your life. How naive I'd been. I'd known nothing of the real world. Nothing of pain or hurt or heartache.

When I saw Jake with that stupid girl at the party all those years ago, I thought it was the worst thing in the world. That was merely a graze in comparison to the gaping hole in my heart I've had to cope with since.

I've always been good at hiding my feelings, burying how I felt. The pain is just bigger now. I have to force it to stay deep in my chest where it can't drown me. I splash my face again, the cold jolting my eyes open and clearing them of the tears on the brink of escaping. I haven't cried in years, and Jake Stewart isn't going to make me now.

I walk back out of the bathroom and pick up my underwear and clothes.

"Where do you think you're going?" his gruff voice questions from the bed.

"Home. This was a mistake."

"No, not this time. You ran off last time. You're not doing it again."

I sit on the edge of the bed and hook my corset up, covering myself from his eyes. My dress is next. I stand and slide my feet into my heels. I look at Jake who's lounging on the bed with a smug look on his face.

"It's not your decision if I stay. See you around." I'm firm and to the point and feel like a complete bitch. This part is usually the easiest. My feet are more hesitant than I wish, but I leave and head for the front door. I grab the handle, but the door doesn't budge. I twist it around and wiggle it, pulling and pushing to try and get it to open. It doesn't.

"What the hell! Let me out," I shout, realising he's locked me in.

"No. Not until we talk."

"Talk? Seriously? Since when do you ever want to talk, Jake?" I storm back into the bedroom. "So, we had good sex. You don't get to keep me here. I want to go home."

"Good sex?" he questions and sits up in bed. His eyes are hard and show the edge that Jake always possessed. "That wasn't just good sex. That was fucking amazing sex, and it doesn't happen all the time, baby. And this isn't just about the sex. What's happened to you? You're not the girl I remember."

I see a flicker of real concern in his eyes, and it knocks my confidence. I need to get out of here. My heart races in my chest as fear and anxiety pump through my body.

"No, and you're not the guy I remember either. He would have kicked me out by now, so how about you open the door."

"What happened between you and Tim? When did you move to London?"

"That's none of your business."

He's up on his feet now, standing off against me. "Yes, it fucking is. I want to understand you. Talk to me."

"No. This was a mistake." I push him backwards, feeling suffocated from his closeness. It was too much. I couldn't talk about the past, not now and not with Jake.

"No, it wasn't and don't fucking lie again. It pisses me off. How did you get those scars? And why won't you talk to me? You were the only person I ever talked to at school." His hands scrunch into balls by his side as we shout at each other.

"Back off, Jake. Leave me alone. This was a mistake, and I don't want to see you again." I march around his imposing frame and around the bedroom, grabbing his trousers from the floor. I search through his pockets for keys and find them. He's on me quickly and wrestles them out of my hand.

"Don't run, Lily. Just, stay. Stay and talk to me."

"No!" I snatch my empty hands away, glaring as viciously as I can at him.

"You're being a bitch. The Lily I knew…"

"The Lily you knew doesn't exist anymore so stop fucking hoping she'll come back. I buried her five years ago, so get over it. This is who I am now. It doesn't matter either way because I won't be seeing you ever again. Don't come looking for me again."

We both pant, our verbal fight as active as a physical one. Fighting with Jake is like sex with Jake. It wakes me up and stirs emotions I had become adept at burying. Blood races through my veins, charging me with energy. Leaving is the only option. He is more dangerous to my health now than when we were kids.

"You're just pissing me off, Lily. Don't. Talk to me and I'll give you the key."

"Fuck you! I don't owe you anything. Forget about me, like you did all those years ago."

"Hey, don't go there."

"Oh, really? You think it's alright to shout and demand answers from me, but can't take it when I tell you the truth."

"It was different then. You were happy. You had Tim. You didn't need me in your life." He turns away and runs his hands through his dishevelled hair.

"So you ran away, didn't answer my messages. Some way to treat a friend. So how about we call it even and you open the fucking door!" I scream. Pressure constricts my chest and the burn of tears singes my throat.

"I kept my distance because I couldn't have you. I couldn't have you like I craved. You were under my fucking skin, Lily. You meant too fucking much to treat you like I treated other girls." His admission is soft like he's embarrassed by what he just said.

I take his moment of distraction to grab the keys. As soon as they're in my hand, I rush to the front door and fumble them in the lock. I get the door open, but Jake's hand slams it shut.

"Don't shut me out. Not now."

"Too late."

"Just, tell me what happened?"

"Tim died. He was killed. Now leave me alone."

His weight comes off the door, and I slip out. I flee in a panic, refusing to look back. I swipe at my eyes, stemming the tears that gather. I break free of his building, and out into the cool of the night. It's still raining, but I don't care. My priority now is to get home and never see Jake again.

JAKE

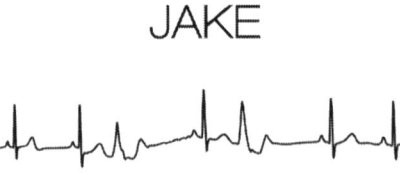

One month later

I'd spent years trying to forget Lily Hill. Finally, I get her under me without the guilt that I feared, and she turns the tables on me. She beat me at my own fucking game, and I didn't even know she was playing me. I'd been a bastard to hundreds of girls over the years. Now I know how it feels.

Tim is dead. Got to admit, I wouldn't have guessed it. It only goes a short way to explain things and without Lily talking to me, I am stuck.

I distract myself with work. Every time I feel the need to go out and get shit-faced, I picture Lily's body wrapped around some arsehole and anger explodes inside my gut, along with the desire to punch something.

I am going to need a new treadmill soon. Sweating the frustration out of my body isn't working, but I don't give up. So far, the three times I'd given in and gone out, I've been so off my face drunk, I couldn't even remember what I did. Nick seems to think I am my usual self, just in a piss-poor mood. *Like I need reminding.*

A loud thumping on my front door halts my pity party.

"Hey. Come on. I need a wingman." Nick barges in before I can shut the door in his face.

"Not in the mood, Nick. You don't need a wingman, anyway. You're perfectly capable of bedding whoever you have your sights on."

"Fine then. You need to get back in the game. You've been off since the girl at Harts. You're either working out or so drunk you don't give a fuck. Where's the fun in that?" Nick tries and fails to hide his agitation. He sniffs every few seconds and his pupils are dilated. I hadn't done coke for a few years. There was no way I was going to risk that at work.

"You're high. Leave the shit alone and go home."

"No, I'm good. Come on man."

Something told me I wasn't going to win this one. "Fine. But no coke. I mean it."

I stomp off to shower and change. It is still early, but it's clear Nick came here with one thing on his mind.

We're out the door in half an hour, my mood no more improved. First stop is a sushi bar where we meet up with some of Nick's usual crowd. We eat, have a few beers, and I attempt to be civil. They all know I'm not one for talking or sharing. The reputation I had at school was an accurate reflection of me and so it stuck into adulthood. I still skated the edge of politeness. Luckily, being a corporate lawyer, I don't need to play nice.

A couple of hours later we're in a booth at Harts. Nick is downing liquor like the bar is going to run dry, but at least he's not snorting lines. He's plying me with alcohol, and my head starts to buzz. It doesn't take the edge off my frustration or my anger at Lily, but I'm coming around to the idea of getting a pretty little thing to help me forget.

An assortment of coloured dresses and heels pack the dance floor, all ripe for the picking. A petite blonde in a green dress more like a belt catches my eye for all the right reasons. Great tits, tiny waist, heels that could stab you through the heart. You could see the shine from her layers of lip gloss from here. I leave the guys to their banter and go and see if the girl lives up to my stereotype assumptions.

She spins and twirls around with her friends, and I make sure she sees me coming. Her smile is as obvious as my mine. She's here to play, and tonight, so am I.

My hands crawl around her waist and pull her back to me. She obliges and grinds her arse right into my crotch. She holds nothing back. At this rate, we'd be fucking on the dance floor. I move my hands up and skim them under her chest and flatten her to me. I give her ear a little nip to see what her reaction is. I wasn't going to go easy on this little thing. I want a hard fuck. I have a memory to rid my mind of. She pulls away but continues to dance. My fingers dig a little harder, but she's all skin and bone, and there is no way those tits are real. She might not be the girl I'm looking for, but she's not saying no.

I grab her jaw and turn her face so I can kiss her. Her bottom lip is pouty, and I'm struck with the vision of her on her knees with my cock down her throat. I grab her hair and tilt her head back to kiss her. Her lips part as I tongue her mouth.

My eyes drift open, and I look past the girl's shoulder.

Lily stands motionless on the dance floor staring at me. Our eyes lock and the next second feels like an hour. Rage hits me like a truck—rage that she left me, didn't return my calls, and rage I still want her. I turn the lip gloss queen in my arms, so Lily has a good look at her. My hand snakes down the front of her dress to her hem and slides underneath as I pull her in close to my lips and kiss her neck. I'm all over her, and she loves the attention. I smear the sticky gloss on my lips over her neck. Her light moans grow desperate as my hand travels higher up her thigh. I remember pulling this same fucking shit on Lily back when we were kids, and the thought kicks me in the stomach. My eyes never leave Lily's, but as I keep watch, I see her eyes change. For a split second, I can see the hurt and vulnerability she's been hiding. Hurt I put there, making her watch what I'm doing. I feel like a teenager again, wanting to get back at her for how she made me feel. I blink and break our connection. It's all the time she needs to flee.

Watching her turn and run is a slap in the face. It was she who never wanted to see me again. So why the fuck should I feel guilty about what I'm doing now? I snatch my hand from underneath the girl's dress and let go of her.

"Hey, what's the matter? It was just getting good," Little Miss Party complains.

"You're not my type," I shout and give her an insincere grin before abandoning the floor.

"Nick, I'm leaving."

"What? What happened? She is perfect for you."

"Like fuck she is. See you at work."

I rush out of the club and scan the entrance. No sign of Lily. I'm not expecting to see her, but I can't help but hope. *Fuck!* I shouldn't feel like this. Acid gnaws at my stomach. I never feel like this, except when Lily is involved.

I shouldn't have done that just to spite her. *How the fuck did I end up here?* The last few weeks have proved until I can get Lily out of my system, I'm going to be piss-poor company. My underlying worry is *can* I get Lily out of my system? I haven't found a way yet. I know she's in pain. I know she's not herself. I let our friendship die. Now I had the opportunity to turn that around. I could be here for her and show her that there is more to me than my sleazy reputation would indicate. I want to help her. I can help her. *God, I'm a bastard.* But I want to do better—for Lily.

LILY

My breath comes in huge gulps as I collapse in the back of the taxi. I'd managed to hold it together until I exited the club, but I could feel my will melting away. For the first time in years, I wanted to give up. It is too hard to wrestle the demons that I can feel under the surface. The guilt, pain and agony that I'd buried has reawakened after years of being shut away in the dark, all because Jake has made me feel… something. My emotions are a living thing inside of me, and I'm desperate to keep them contained until I'm alone. I can't break here.

I plunge my teeth into my bottom lip to stifle the cry that has risen in my throat. Thankfully, the journey is short. I bolt from the car as soon as I've paid. I race up to my apartment and slam the door behind me.

My tears burn as they fall and I cry. Loud, guttural screams echo around my head as my emotions smash their way out. I can cope with the numb state I'd put myself in. This isn't numb.

My heart ached in my chest as if Jake had torn out a chunk and kept it for himself. And why should I be so upset about him? It shouldn't matter to me. I told him I didn't want to see him again. Seeing him kiss that girl was the first thing that affected me since Tim—as if my grief and guilt has been encased in ice, and Jake provided the heat to thaw those feelings.

I watched my boyfriend die in front of me, trapped, as the blood drained from his body and he slipped away. I watched, helpless as he died. I'd never felt as distraught or as utterly useless as I did that evening. My pain intensified as he slipped away. On top of that, when I woke up they told me there were complications with the surgery on my pelvis which meant that I couldn't have children. My surgery didn't go according to plan and they had to perform a hysterectomy. I lost my entire future. Seeing the man I used to have feelings for kiss someone shouldn't even register as a blip on my radar. *But it did.* The last five years flashed in front of my eyes. My recovery, moving, cutting ties, starting a new life and turning into someone that I wouldn't have recognised back then. I couldn't cope with the rage and the emptiness that consumed me after the accident, so I shut it off. I chose not to care. It was my coping mechanism. Jake had knocked through the damn, and I was drowning in the flood.

My body shivers and my eyes peel open.

I remember crying until exhausted. I must have fallen asleep on the floor. My limbs feel like they're lined with lead, but I drag myself up. The sky is still pitch black outside my windows. I go to the kitchen, pull a glass off the drainer and fill it with water. I swallow half the glass and take the few steps needed to cross from the kitchen to the lounge. I curl up in the armchair and pull my knees to my chest.

I've been living in a bubble for years. It was a carefully constructed world that enabled me to function and get through the day and lead a life. I used my behaviour as a shield against the grief and loss I refused to deal with. Tim and I hadn't even thought about children, not really. Being told that I would never be able to have babies made me miss something I didn't even realise I wanted. How could I be so devastated over a scenario that hadn't happened?

My heart flutters in my chest and I hold my hand over my stomach as I wait for the wave of pain to ebb away. As I squeeze my eyes closed and clench my teeth together, I hope that the empty nothingness I'm used to will replace this invasion of feelings soon.

Scattered images flash before my eyes as I fight to gain control of my thoughts. Jake when we were at school, Tim's face when we first met. His image morphs into the one that haunted my dreams for weeks as I lay in the hospital bed. Blood stained, pale and still. Tim is who I should be falling apart for. He's the one who meant something to me, who I loved, who I shared a life with. Jake shouldn't have this power over me. He's fractured the world I was okay with and let the darkness creep in, swirling around me like smoke.

No matter how tight I press my eyes, my cheeks are wet with tears, and I slap the moisture from them, punishing my stupid behaviour. I rest my head against the chair and try and find some calm amongst the rampaging emotions. I concentrate on my breathing—the steady in and out—as something to focus on and grab control. I can do that.

A few hours later, I wake with a stiff neck. Light flickers in through the windows. It's morning. I peel myself out of the chair and trudge to the bathroom. I set the shower running and strip out of my clothes, tossing them aside. The water is soothing, but I don't want that. I want the heat to burn away the memories that have escaped from my carefully constructed box. My hand twists the temperature until the heat scalds my skin. The physical pain dulls the emotional ache, and I'm thankful.

In the past, my feelings bubbled up, like air pockets rising to the surface and venting. But I could always shake them off. Jake had cracked a fissure through me, right down to my core. It felt impossible to repair it.

The heat fogs the small shower enclosure, and finally, I can't take the searing heat. I step out of the shower and steam follows, billowing out as I grab for the towel. When I'm dry, I head to my room and open my wardrobe to find some clothes to shove on. My fingers travel over my collection of garments, but all I see is the reckless, slutty behaviour I adopted. Everything is a reflection of the woman I've become to hide from my grief. Fresh, hot tears run down my cheeks as a stream of images of me with nameless men invade my mind.

My hands grab hold of the clothes that were my personal uniform, and I tear them from the rail, throwing them to the ground with as much force as I can muster. Rage fills my veins and strengthens my actions as I grab and fling clothes to the floor. These strips of black hid a part of me that I was happy to forget. They offered me the chance to behave with no questions or conscience. Now, it sickens my stomach.

Shame crawls over me as I think back over how I acted. The girl that Tim fell in love with would never have acted so brash and cheap. I hated girls like me. I leave the wreckage on the floor and settle on a plain t-shirt I usually sleep in and a pair of leggings. I escape the room and go back to the lounge.

I look around my apartment, and the rage dissolves as sorrow bubbles up in my chest. My home is a plain, small box that holds no sentiment or personality. The walls are a non-descript cream, the carpets and furnishings are a rainbow of neutral tones. The surfaces are empty, with nothing to show who I am or what I like. The apartment might be mine on paper, it might be where I sleep and live, but there is nothing that makes this place a home.

My body drops down into the armchair again, and I hold my phone in my hands. I scroll through the numbers in my phone, flicking my index finger over the screen. My mum and dad, Charlotte and Jake are all still listed although I've not called. Leaving meant cutting ties. At the time, all I could think of was escaping the pain of my memories. I wanted out, and that meant out of everything that was my life.

I continue scrolling until I see Tim's name. I couldn't bring myself to delete it. My finger hovers over the letters. A tear drops onto the screen, obscuring his name. "I'm sorry. I'm so sorry."

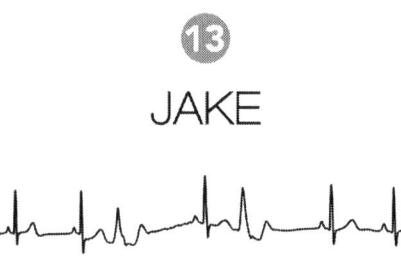

JAKE

Two weeks later

Lily isn't easy to find. She must be the only person in the world not on Facebook. I can't track her down through old friends because I didn't keep in contact with any of the people from school. Andy doesn't count. He is my brother, although there was a time I considered him more of a friend than a relation.

Two weeks of work, running and attempting to find Lily Hill are dragging on me. I've not been out, had a drink or touched another woman and I feel like my insides will explode if I don't do something soon. Lily is becoming an obsession, and part of me likes that, I feed off the energy I create. A darker part of me worries that nothing will quench my need for her. Lily has driven me to visit home. I can't stand being stuck in London where no one knows her.

My family aren't my favourite people, but I tolerate Andy when he wants to escape and blow off steam. He was my first role model, so to speak. It is no surprise that even though he is married, he likes to play the field. Doesn't stop him from gloating about his perfect family at family lunches with Mum and Dad.

I stayed away, happy to construct a life away from the second-rate brother status I'd been slapped with as a teen. I don't need anyone from my past. Except now. I have to swallow my pride and go looking for answers. Charlotte is the only friend of Lily's who I can remember. She is also the only one I can find on Facebook and conveniently she still lives in Bristol.

I can't remember what Charlotte looks like. I have her profile picture to go on, but that's about it. We agree to meet in a coffee shop at the top of Park Street in Bristol. It's crowded with students and people out for their fix of caffeine.

I'd stayed in a hotel last night, not ready for a cosy evening with Mum and Dad. I check my watch and try to rein back my annoyance. Charlotte is late. I drink my coffee and remember why I'm here and why I'm doing this. I want to help Lily. I need to understand her.

"Jake?"

I turn to see a tall, slender woman with beautifully silky blond hair looking at me.

"Yes. Charlotte?" I stand to greet her, and she takes her seat.

"God, you've not changed at all. Well, not really. How are you?"

"I'm fine thanks. I appreciate you agreeing to meet me."

"No trouble. I'm surprised you remember me actually. You mentioned you wanted help with something?"

"Yes. Can I get you a drink first? Coffee, tea?"

"A decaf latte please."

"Sure." I go and place an order and head back to Charlotte. I rack my brains for a memory of her. *Did I sleep with her?* I shove that thought aside and stick to the plan.

"Here you go."

"Thanks, so you don't live locally? When did you move away?"

"No, this is just a passing visit." I'm not here to 'catch up' and want to cut to the reason I'm here. "So, I'm hoping you have Lily's number." I open with the easy stuff.

"Lily? Lily Hill?" she looks puzzled.

"Yes, you were friends with her in school."

"I know, and I remember you two being friends, sort of."

"Do you have her number?"

"Only her old one. I don't think she's using it anymore." She rummages in the cavernous bag she pulls into her lap. She pulls out her phone and taps the screen a few times. "Here." She slides it across the table, and I look at the digits. It's the same number I have.

"Thanks. Why do you say her old number?"

"Well, we're not in touch anymore. It's sad."

"Would you mind telling me what happened? I know Tim died." I want to push for details.

"You've seen her? Recently?" Her eyes flash to mine, and I can't mistake the hope I see.

"Yes, she's in London."

"No one's heard from her for years. She just upped and vanished. When did you see her? Is she alright? How is she?"

Worry and concern etch Charlotte's expression, and I feel relief that I'm not the only one who thinks Lily's behaviour is unusual.

"I met up with her a few weeks ago. Can you fill in the blanks?"

"It must have been about five years ago now. She and Tim were in an awful car accident. Someone smashed at high speed into the driver's side. The car was crushed between other bigger cars on the motorway. It took longer than usual for the emergency crews to arrive and they had to cut Lily and Tim out of the car. Tim died at the scene, and Lily was hospitalised for months. She was too badly hurt to attend his funeral. We all went to visit of course, but she refused to talk to us. She shut everyone out. It was horrible. It was as if Lily had died in that accident as well as Tim."

"What about her parents?"

"I went around there a few times. Lily wouldn't see them either." When she was released from the hospital, she just disappeared. Her parents didn't know where she went. She cut all ties with people. I don't think she's been back to Bristol since." Charlotte's face drops to her coffee and she cradle's it against her for a few moments.

"Thank you." I need to get out of here. I knew Tim had died. I *hadn't* known Lily had been injured. From the sound of things, she could have died. I try and imagine how I would feel in a world without Lily.

I stand up to leave.

"What? Is that it?" Charlotte looks confused.

"I'm sorry. I appreciate what you've told me."

"Wait… will you at least let me know if you get in touch with her again?"

"Sure. I have your details." I leave the coffee shop and slide into the flow of human traffic walking up the hill. Charlotte had filled in some of the blanks, and although I hated what I had found out, I needed more. I was beginning to understand why I don't recognise Lily. She really isn't the same person anymore. I push harder to reach the street where I'd parked my car. Lily's parents don't live in town. I will stop in and see them before facing my parents.

Twenty minutes later I'm standing in front of Lily's old house. *This is crazy.* In the space of a couple of months, I've gone from trying to forget this girl to becoming obsessed with finding out more about her. Every time I toyed with the idea of going back to pretending she didn't exist, I picture her face, I hear her cries, and I feel her body wrapped around mine. I take a deep breath and knock on her parent's door.

A tall man in his early sixties I guess, answers. He has the same eyes as Lily. "Hello?"

"Hi, I'm Jake. I was a friend of Lily's. You probably don't remember me."

"I'm afraid she doesn't live here anymore."

"I know. I was hoping I could talk to you."

He scrutinises me for a moment before he opens the door wider. I step into the hall and take a few steps towards the living room. I think I only came here a couple of times back in school.

"Jane! We have a visitor. Go on, through you go."

I feel like a teenager again, rather than the man I am today. I sit on one of the chairs in the lounge and wait for Lily's mum to join us.

An older version of Lily walks into the room and stops when she sees me.

"Hi, Mrs. Hill. I'm Jake. I'm a friend of Lily's."

"Jake, she talked about you. What can we do for you?"

"I'm trying to get back in contact with Lily."

Her face softens, and I see the pain in her eyes.

"I'm afraid we haven't spoken to her for a while. We can't help you there." She walks towards her husband and leans on his shoulder. It's an intimate move that makes me think of being close to someone, how it would feel to seek comfort from another.

"I met up with Lily a few weeks ago. I was hoping you had a number…"

"You've seen her? Recently?" The shock on Jane's face is visible.

"Yes. Just briefly."

"How is she? *Where* is she? We've not seen her for years." At that admission, she takes a seat next to her husband and clasps her hands around his.

Charlotte had told me that she cut off ties and moved. I just didn't expect it to have lasted for so long or included her parents.

"She's in London. Shoreditch, or at least that's where I saw her. Twice."

Tears shine on Jane's face.

"What do you know about Lily, Jake?" her dad asks, and I know he's deciding how much to tell me.

"I know she was in an accident. That Tim died." I keep my answer brief. I don't think they'll be able to help me find her again, but I want to hear what they have to say.

"Lily's pelvis was crushed in the accident. It took several surgeries and a lot of time in the hospital to get her walking again. She had her recovery to concentrate on, and I'm thankful for that. She shut out everything else. Even us. After she was out of the hospital and back on her feet, she disappeared. She put her house up for sale and didn't come back. We get a card for birthdays and Christmas. She told us that she needed to be on her own and that she knew where we were. Apart from that, we've not seen her."

I turn away from his face, not able to look at his eyes any longer. A sombre silence falls over us as we all take in the words that were said.

"I'm very sorry, Mr. and Mrs. Hill. If I see Lily again, I'll try and get her to contact you." I stand up and move towards the door. This has to be awkward for all of us. I feel like I've come in here to offer them some sort of hope at reaching their daughter again and all I've done is drag up the painful past.

Pushing open the front door to my family home shouldn't feel this weird. I don't feel like I should just walk in, but I do.

"Hello!" I call. I'd phoned early on to say I'd be dropping in so at least they were expecting me.

"We're in the living room," Mum calls.

I walk through the hallway and into the spacious room. It's brighter than I remember. Perhaps new furniture.

"Hi, Jake. Come in, come in.

"You have perfect timing, Jake. Andy and Lisa have just told us that they're expecting. Isn't that wonderful?" She practically beams with joy as she delivers this news.

"Congratulations." I nod in the direction of Andy. He's sitting in one of the plush new sofas looking smug, with his wife next to him, and from within me, the urge to wipe the smile from his face rears its nasty head. Though I've not seen my folks for the best part of a year, they hardly acknowledge my presence. Andy and his news of grandchildren has taken centre court.

God, I sound like a needy prick. "We're going out to celebrate this evening. We couldn't let the occasion slip past. I'm sure we could add you to the table. It is your brother, after all."

"No thank you. It's just a flying visit. I'll be on my way soon." The last thing I want to watch is another gloat fest over Andy.

"Okay, well it's nice to see you. I'll put the kettle on. You've got time for a quick cup?"

"Sure."

"So, what's life like in the city? Keeping yourself busy?" Andy makes an effort at polite conversation.

"It's fine. I'm busy at work."

"And why did you leave that law firm again? Seems like it was a step down for you?"

"Setting up and administrating a corporate team at a multinational business is hardly a step-down. Perhaps you're a little out of touch?" I quip.

"Hardly," he scoffs. "Of course, now that we have a family to think about, we'll have to move to a bigger house, perhaps closer to Mum and Dad." He lands that piece of news perfectly as Mum walks in with a tray of tea.

"Where's Dad?" I ask.

"He'll be back for lunch. If you stay you might catch him?"

"No, I need to get back." *Before I explode.* "Are you seeing anyone, Jake?" Lisa asks as Mum hands out the tea.

"Not at the moment."

"Not back with Yvonne?" Andy smirks, and I send him a cold hard stare in response.

"I was never with Yvonne."

"Oh, I don't think she sees it that way." Andy's grin brings back everything I hate about him. "She is such a *nice* girl." He smiles like the cocky shit he is, wrapping his arm around Lisa. Something about his righteous attitude makes me wonder if he's seen Yvonne recently.

The room falls silent, and I drink my tea in peace. I'll never be comfortable around my family. I'm not wired that way. I wonder if my folks would have the same pained and haunted look on their faces if I cut them from my life like Lily had. Probably not. *God, I'm a bastard.*

LILY

The pain won't go away. I thought that if I let some of it out, if I acknowledged part of what I'd been feeling, then I'd be able to cope with it, learn to control it like I did in the past. That turned out to be a ridiculous idea.

Thoughts of my handsome Tim and the fairy-tale life we lived together, my career as a physiotherapist that brought me such joy and all my closest friends flood unchecked into my mind. Memories of the past possess me. I fled the pain and grief of those reminders like a wounded animal and threw myself into a frantic attempt to fill my days with a mindless job and drunken, sexual excess. It had worked—for a while. It had worked until Jake.

I resent him for waking me up. I've been sleepwalking through life, and suddenly I have to deal with the all the unresolved pain and grief that I hoped to escape by leaving Bristol.

I've made swimming a part of my routine. I'd taken it up during rehab and found it gave me peace. My mind shuts off when I swim—all I concentrate on are the steady repetitive strokes of my arms and legs. I can't sleep, so I'm up at the crack of dawn to swim before getting into work. My mind switches gears at my desk, focusing on the tasks at hand before I go back to the gym in the evening to do some general fitness. In order to fall asleep, I have to be shattered. Even then, I achieve only a restless sleep. The nightmares are less predictable, but I've been living on patchy sleep for so long now, I've forgotten what a good night sleep felt like.

I haven't been back out to the clubs. Since my little breakdown, neither my mind nor my body wants to re-visit one of my coping mechanisms. Plus, I'm not ready to run the risk of seeing Jake again. Part of me thinks it's ridiculous to imagine I'd run into him again. It was completely by accident the first time. But my heart can't take that risk. Not yet, when I'm still feeling so raw. He's turned my feelings back on.

JAKE

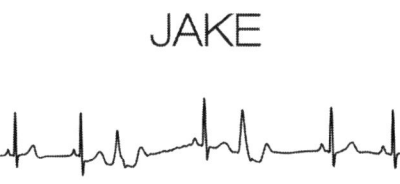

Two weeks later

I'm going fucking crazy. I'd gone back to Harts and XO with no luck. Not really surprising, but I must find her. All I have to do is close my eyes, and I can see her, taste her. My obsession is well and truly developed.

I know she lives in and around Shoreditch, so my next move puts me well into stalker territory. I pull up google and search. I skim and click on the website that will hopefully deliver me closer to knowing where she is. I type her name and Shoreditch and wait. Two results return with address details for 'L' or 'Lily Hill' in 'Shoreditch'. My fingers fly across the keyboard, searching for addresses. They aren't far from my place, a fifteen-minute walk, max.

For the rest of the afternoon my temper is put to the test. I'm asked some stupid fucking questions from the finance department, and I have to endure a monthly review session from the risk analysis department. Every atom of my being itches to get out of here. I'm first out the door when the monthly review ends.

Both addresses that popped up on my computer search are in apartment blocks, so I pick the one closest to my address first.

Shoreditch matches my lifestyle and my interests and demonstrates that I have money. My two-bedroom apartment is small, but the mortgage is anything but. Most of the people I know can't afford a studio apartment around here, let alone anything bigger. It is the first thing I wanted when I signed my employment contract with my new company.

I find a coffee shop conveniently located on the opposite side of the road to the address. I can see people come and go from the apartment building. Its red-brick exterior makes the building look older than a lot of the other residences. The street has a steady trickle of people heading home from work. Every time I see a girl with brown hair, my heart rushes to life, only to crash back to reality.

After my second coffee, I ask myself, *what the hell am I doing?* The frustration and anger that has been eating me up for the last few weeks is growing unbearable. This act of idiocy doesn't help. I finish the coffee and head back outside. I stare at the apartment entrance before turning and heading back to the station.

A flash of deep chestnut catches my eye, and I turn to watch a woman still in running gear and carrying a gym bag as she walks toward the building on the other side of the road. It's Lily.

LILY

My arms stretch out and pull through the water sending tiny bubbles through my fingers. My rhythm is steady and sure, and I count the strokes; one, two, breathe repeat. The water naturally blocks out any sounds and quiets my mind. The focus on making my body work in a coordinated way helps to stop other thoughts from encroaching.

If I could swim with my eyes closed, then I'd be able to shut everything out. The water cocoons me, keeping me safe in my own little bubble. I spend a few minutes floating with my eyes closed at the end of my swim. These minutes are the most peaceful of my day and I always wish for longer before I have to get out and ready for work.

My shower is quick and efficient, and I towel off and blow dry my hair before pulling it back into a messy bun. I slide into my work wear and leave the changing rooms. It's still early as I walk towards the station, but the streets are already filling with people on their way to work. London and the morning rush hour is a horrible mix.

"Hi."

I spin around to see Jake walking by my side, a grin on his face telling me he's pleased to see me or pleased he's shocked me.

"Hi," I reply, mortified that he's walking next to me. I pull my bag tighter against my body making sure I'm as together as I can be. I keep my stride and try to pick up my pace.

"Are you going to run away from me now as well?"

I look at him trying to judge what he's after. I halt, and he walks a few feet in front before turning back to face me.

"No. I'm not running. I'm going to work. How did you find me? I thought I made it clear I didn't want to see you again." I continue on my path, determination in my steps while inside I'm falling apart.

"You did, but I chose to ignore it. I don't want us to go our separate ways."

"Tough."

He keeps step with me. I risk a glance at him from the corner of my eye. That was a bad idea. He's still smiling, his hazel eyes look soft and kind. It hurtles me back to when we were at school. When he would walk me part of the way to class, trying to talk to me rather than ignore me. My fist wraps around the strap of my bag, and I pull it in closer.

"Please, Jake. I can't do this. I'm going to work. Leave me alone." My eyes lock with the pavement, scared to look at him again. My heart races in my chest and my body buzzes from the hit of adrenaline it just took. My eyes slide to the side to catch another glimpse of Jake, but he's not there. I stop and look around but in the few feet I've marched on, he's vanished.

I push the disappointment away and get on with my task at hand. I need to get to work. Jake is messing about. There isn't anything deeper to this. My emotions are getting the better of me. It's another coincidence he ran into me. He lives close by. That's all. It doesn't mean anything.

Hope should be the last thing to rise at the thought of seeing Jake again. I've told myself I can't see him again. I'm not ready to consider another relationship. I'm working on my past behaviour now that I can't escape the reality I've found myself in. Jake stopped me in my tracks and shone a bright light on me. He'd given me the jolt to examine my actions, and I had, through big sad tears. I can't slink back into the shadows now. I need to work through my unresolved grief. I buried that along with all the pain and heartache. I should have grieved properly. But how am I to do that with Jake pulling at my fragile heart?

Jake has become my personal stalker. For the last couple of weeks, he's been a regular on my journey to work. In the morning, he waits outside the gym for me to finish my swim; he walks me down the street to the station. He even has a cup of coffee waiting for me. He is sneaking his way into my heart again. He shows up with a regularity I'm beginning to enjoy. He's always looked handsome, but seeing him as the thirty-something man he is now, is more than my delicate heart can take. His suits fit his broad physique and gives a professional slant to the bad boy I've always seen him as. His hair is neat, setting off his firm jaw and warm eyes. The Jake package is hard to ignore when you see it so regularly.

"How long before you start talking to me?" He cuts in front of my path, stalling my march to work and my daydream.

My eyes don't lift to meet his. I step to walk around him, but he grabs my shoulders and holds me.

"This is bollocks. Would it hurt so much to have a coffee with me, instead of walking away all the time? I promise to be on my best behaviour."

His face is stern. I close my eyes and summon some inner strength I know is locked away for emergencies. "Jake, I'm not ready to see you, not the way you're suggesting. You've stormed into my world and shaken me up." I search his eyes, and hope he will understand. This is the most honest I've been with him since yelling in his face all those weeks ago.

"Don't you think you've done the same to me?" Anger lights up his face. "You played me. You fucked me and left without a word. I deserve more than that from you."

I cringe at his words. "This isn't a great place to talk, Jake." I look around at the busy street, as people part to flow around us on their way to wherever they are going.

"Well, considering you won't talk, I don't have much choice, do I?"

Snakes of desire shiver down my spine. Jake's stance, his words, everything about him in this minute, tells my body it doesn't need space or time; all it needs is him. I duck my head and step to the side. This time, Jake's hands slide from my shoulders, and I continue my walk. Every time I see Jake, it gets harder to pretend that my heart doesn't come alive at the thought of us together. I can't. I'm not ready.

I'm distracted for the rest of the day. Every time the door to the lobby swings open my eyes shoot up from my desk to see if it is Jake. The day drags on, and I wish I didn't feel remorse or sorrow at how I treated Jake, or how I feel about him. I wish I was just a normal girl who can have feelings for a guy without complications and have fun. But I'm not a normal girl and Jake's not just a guy. As for fun? I turn the word over and try to wrap my tongue around it. There hadn't been much fun for a while. Five o'clock comes around, and I gladly sign-out and pick up my gym bag. As it's a Friday, it takes nearly an hour to reach the gym and part of me just wants to skip it and fall into bed. I haven't taken sleeping tablets since shortly after the accident, but I know two little pills will put me out for the count. I never wanted to take them, but it became necessary with my growing insomnia and nightmares. I've been able to sleep quite peacefully the last few weeks. It isn't the nightmares keeping me awake.

My feet stop outside of the pharmacy on the main shopping street, but I don't go in. I force my body forward and around the corner to the gym. I open the door, sign in and head to the changing rooms. I emerge and head to the cardio room to warm up. It's busy considering it's a Friday evening. The treadmills are full. A tall, muscled guy whose body forms one of those inverted triangles, slows and stops his run. I can see his back moving in and out as he waits to catch his breath. Hairs on the back of my neck stand to attention, and Jake turns around and jumps off the machine. The sweat coating his toned arms turns his body into a glistening shrine for women to worship.

His eyes catch me staring, and I duck away, embarrassed I was caught admiring the display.

"Wait, Lily. Stop," Jake calls after me, and I pause and slowly turn. He's scowling.

"Just so we're clear, you might want to deny anything happened between us. I don't. I haven't stopped thinking of you in fifteen years. I'm not going to start now. I'll wear you down until you give in. And you will. Enjoy your run."

He walks out of the room. My heart stammers against my ribs as if I've already run ten miles. I sit on a nearby weight machine, lost. Confusion wraps my mind. Jake and I used to be friends. It might not have been a conventional friendship, but it was one I clung to, desperate to ensure it survived. Seeing him, being with him, has stirred the fond memories I had of school and uni and of being hopeful for the future. There is a way forward for both of us, and I cling to that as I finish up in the gym and get changed. I'd lost so much over the last few years. Did I want to carry on down that road? I will apologise to him. We'll go for a coffee. Nothing has to happen. It will simply be two old friends catching up. As I run my plan over in my mind, I find myself questioning my conviction on the last point. Suddenly, I want to call him and I hurry out of the gym.

"Hi." Jake startles me as I exit and turn towards home.

"Jake! What are you doing?"

"Waiting for you."

"Answer one question for me. Why, after *you* cut off everything between us years ago, do you want back in now? I don't get it?" It's the one question I could never answer when I found myself reminiscing about the past. "We fucked a couple times. It doesn't put us in a relationship." He eyes me silently, his expression inscrutable, and all my uncertainties and fears flood back. With a growl, I storm off towards the building I call home.

"Don't you want to know why?" he calls after me.

"Yes," I shout back, still on track for home. His steps fall into pace beside mine, and we walk in silence the ten minutes it takes to reach home. I take the stairs up to my floor and still don't stop him. I've not invited anyone back here. I don't have friends and the guys that I sleep with never ask to stay.

I pause at my door and look at him. His hazel eyes turn darker in the dim hallway, and for a moment, I'm scared of what he might say.

"The reason I'm not giving up now is because the Lily I knew wouldn't pick me up in a bar and let me fuck her." His eyes bore into mine, heating me from the inside as if molten lava runs through my veins instead of blood. "She wouldn't let me treat her that way. She wouldn't run out on me and treat me as if what we felt for each other didn't mean anything."

I open the door and break the spell. I barge in and hear Jake slam it behind him.

"I told you, I'm not the same girl you used to know," I mutter quietly. "If that's who you've come after, then you'll be disappointed." Pain grates at my heart that he won't like the person I've turned into. Right now, I don't like her very much either.

"I want to find out what happened to her. And I'd like to get to know you." His voice softens and pin-prick sensations scatter over my neck and rush down my back.

"Would you like a drink?" I offer. It's a small gesture I hope will discharge the tension between us. I want to grab onto hope and not dwell on the bad stuff. We both need to move on.

"Yes. Anything cold would be great."

JAKE

Thank fuck! I let go of the breath I've been holding. It has been a long couple of weeks, but that time gave me a purpose. I had something to clutch on to, instead of driving myself mad. Seeing Lily so often is a good test of my willpower. So far, I haven't slammed her against the nearest hard surface to kiss her senseless. Of course, my mind doesn't stop at her lips. The images of her coming around my cock play out in techni-fucking-colour.

I watch her move into the small kitchen space and pull a can of Coke out of the fridge. Her place is small. A neat box. Unsurprising as the prices here are ludicrous. Her place is little more than a studio apartment. She pours it into a glass and offers both to me. I take them from her, and she goes to sit in a comfy looking armchair in the corner of the living space. I struggle to sit next to her on the small sofa. It's tiny. Since it's Lily, I'm happy with the lack of personal space.

She pulls her knees up to her chest and balances the can on her knee cap. She's staring at the can and not looking at me. As I watch her, I try to see the girl that used to sneak glances at me in class when she thought I wasn't looking. There is an ocean of pain and past between us. I can feel it weighing heavy on Lily. I tap down the burning sense of possession and protection I feel.

She still ties me in knots. The need I feel for this girl is greater now than ever. When I look at her like this, a little lost and uncertain, I want to wrap her up and protect her and take away all the pain she's been through. "So, did you want to talk about anything specific or are you happy to sit and drink?"

Her voice is calm and matter of fact. She doesn't know I went back home and found out about her from Charlotte and her folks.

"How long have you been in London?"

"Just over four years."

"What are you doing now? It doesn't look like you're a physio any longer."

"No. I gave that up. What about you? Still a lawyer?"

"I head up the legal division of an international company. It was a great promotion for me."

"Congratulations. I take it there isn't someone special in your life."

"Well, it depends on how you define special."

She looks at me, and her cheeks tinge with pink.

"Will you give me your number? I'd like to see you again, and I'd prefer to know how to contact you without having to stalk." I smile at the comment. I have been a bastard over the last few weeks, but it got me what I wanted. *Like it always did.*

"My number's the same."

"So, you received my texts and calls?"

"Yes."

She looks shy as she admits that. My teeth grind together. If she would have just answered her damn phone, we could have avoided the last couple of weeks.

"Will you answer me this time?"

"Yes. As long as you don't turn stalker on me again. That pissed me off. You didn't give me a choice. You took that away."

That was the whole fucking point. She wanted to forget what we did and pass it off. Not going to happen.

"I won't stalk anymore unless you break off our contact again. I might have let you do all the work on our friendship in the past, but not now. I'm going to fight for you, Lily." I take a few swallows of the Coke and get comfy on the sofa. In the past, I would have left by now. How things change.

"This feels weird. We can't go back to how things were before." She looks up, and I see a depth of sadness hidden within them. The blue is dark, dull with pain. I want her bright eyes back.

"I don't want to undo anything we've done. I couldn't forget you when I didn't know what you felt like under me. I certainly don't want to forget you now."

Lily doesn't seem to appreciate my comment and abruptly stands and paces back to the kitchen. I wait for her to come back. After chasing her for weeks, I've finally gained ground. I don't want to scare her off by pushing too much too soon. Sure enough, she reappears, pacing the few feet around the living room like a restless animal.

"So, how do we go about being friends? We've both changed. It's not like we're sixteen anymore."

"We talk; we go out; you tell me your troubles, and I tell you mine." I leave out the part where I want to ravage her. I'm not going to fuck this up again. She doesn't answer, but her feet have brought her back to the chair.

"I haven't had a friend in a long time. I don't think I'm very good at it anymore," she admits quietly.

"I don't think I've ever been a good friend. But you have been, you just need to remember."

Lily finally looks at me. She's scared. She doesn't want to remember, and I think that's part of her 'up and disappear' trick. But I wasn't going to let that get in our way.

I had zero-fucking experience with building a friendship. I never had to work at it because I never needed a friend. My gut told me all the way home that I have to do the hard part now. I just hope I don't fuck it up and Lily comes to realise my bad side is the only side I have. *God, I'm a bastard.*

15
LILY

A date. I'm going on a date with Jake Stewart. He wouldn't take no for an answer. I think of him, picture him, and a smile brightens my face, then fear spears me. Wounds hurt. I have first-hand experience of that. But will sacrificing any future happiness help me?

Maybe what I need is someone to help guide the way back to normality. The little glimmer of light at the end of the tunnel I'd been stuck in for years, is now growing brighter. More than that, I cling to it like a life raft. It isn't like I am moving on with my life the way things are now. Facing my fears could be good. Back at school, I dreamt of going on a date with Jake. It still seems surreal. After everything we'd done together, after so much time and so many life altering events, we're finally standing in line for popcorn. It seems like something kids would do, and part of that is charming.

Awkward gaps fill our conversation, as if we don't know how to just *be* around each other. Even the slight awkwardness reminds me of times at school when I didn't know what to say to him that wouldn't betray my feelings, or he just acted like he didn't want to be around me.

His hand on the base of my back, guiding me forward meant more than words could. It made up for the strained atmosphere between us.

I'd spent the last few weeks in a downward spiral, convincing myself I couldn't be around this man. Openly agreeing to see him was… hard. It still hurts when I look at him, but this pain I can take.

Jake guides me through to the screen, and we take our seats in the theatre. It is some Marvel super-hero film I have no real interest in, but it was Jake's suggestion. The lights dim around us.

I spend the entire film waiting for him to put his arm around me or take hold of my hand. He doesn't, and I am confused and frustrated in equal measure, which only adds to my frustration. This man makes my head spin and throws me back into being a sixteen-year-old again.

His hand drops to the small of my back once more as we move out of the cinema. It is a short tube ride home, but we've barely uttered a word to one another. Things were easier when I could be cross at him for turning up at my door or the gym. I could hold on to my annoyance to get me through. I don't have that excuse now. This man has cut through the numbness I've felt, the emptiness and disregard I've shown myself and made me feel again.

"You've been quiet."

"So have you," I reply.

"It was a pretty lame date."

"Yep." I wasn't going to pretend with him.

"What would you normally do with a friend?"

"What do you mean?"

"What do you normally do when you see friends. What do you do?"

"I don't have any friends right now. I drink a fair amount. I fuck. I don't want to make friends."

We continue heading in the direction of his building, and the conversation dies. With every step closer, I consider if I'm doing the right thing. My mind feels like it's working overtime, but it keeps coming up with the same answer. I want to be with Jake despite the hurt it caused me in the past. I have to see this through and work at finding happiness. A better life.

Jake was so raw, so single-minded with me when things got physical. It was what I needed, but our relationship has shifted again now. This isn't just another hook up for me. I care with Jake and that makes this moment such a big deal. We walk up to the entrance of the building and Jake takes my hand the rest of the way to his door. We still haven't spoken. I'm afraid my voice will betray how nervous I am. This isn't the game I play. I was confident and assured of myself when I met Jake at the club. It was familiar and easy to act the part with him. Now, my armour is crushed at my feet, and I'm vulnerable to everything that is Jake.

As soon as he puts his hands on me, I relax. I don't want to, but it's as if he turns down the noise in my head with just his touch. The fear disappears. He's slow and steady with his movements as if he doesn't want to spook me. Like it or not, he's awakened me. I've seen the woman I've become, and I know I can't keep acting that way.

His fingers trail down my hair and rest, cradling my head. Each move holds purpose like he's reassuring me. His feet nudge closer to me, and his hazel eyes hold the warmth I've been missing for so long.

Soft, welcoming lips brush over mine, and I turn to mush in his arms. The bad boy, mean Jake was dangerous. This caring version of Jake will slay me.

I haven't been exposed emotionally to someone since Tim. Anonymous sex and drinking has been my shield, but there is a yearning growing stronger within me to let go of my defences and not hold back with Jake. I'm on the brink of falling apart, and the only person who can save me is Jake.

His kisses pull me in deeper, and I slip under his spell. All the fight, all the arguments fade away, and I'm left standing in his room. I let him take the lead. I surrender to him, and it's terrifying. I focus on the warmth of his lips, and my arms pull him in close to me.

Our bodies bump against each other, fighting to rid any space between us. The slow and gentle evaporates to leave the lust and passion that had always erupted between us. His clean-washed scent, his strong biceps, his taste, overwhelms my senses. I feel too hot in my clothes. They're too tight. I want to feel Jake's bare skin pressed up against mine, the trail of his lips on my neck and breasts.

I weave my fingers through his hair and cling to him. He lifts me, and I wrap my legs around his waist. He carries me the few feet to the bed and sits down with me in his lap. I pull myself as close as I can and wiggle down against his crotch.

"Stop it, or you'll regret it," his warning is tight and harsh and does nothing to persuade me to cease. I roll my hips and push my body up against him, arching my back as I do.

He flips me so fast I gasp and look up at him in surprise.

"I warned you." He towers over me and makes short work of his jeans and shirt. I push my own jeans down, and Jake grabs the ankles and pulls them off. My shirt is next, but I don't make an attempt to take off my boy-shorts and bustier. I might want our skin against each other, but I wasn't ready to face questions over my scars.

Jake crawls onto the bed, and my whole body trembles with anticipation. He straddles my hips and seats his—very naked, very gorgeous—body over me. His hand cups my cheek and his finger trails down between my breasts before he palms his thick shaft and gives it several leisurely pulls. I watch, transfixed. This isn't like the Jake I've seen so far. He would normally take and demand.

"You're thinking too much, baby. I don't want you to think— unless it's about all the sinful things I'm going to do with you; how good I'm going to make you feel and how hard I'm going to make you come."

My chest rises higher as I take a deep lungful of air.

"There are so many possibilities for you." His eyes home in on mine, and I struggle to see the warm mix of brown and green from his pupils. "If you were just another girl, I might give you my dick to eat before pushing you down on your front and taking your arse. But I don't want that with you. I already know you're fucking amazing. I want more tonight, and I'm not going to be satisfied until you're screaming my name."

My core weeps at his words, and I close my eyes, not wanting to see the feelings he's expressed in words written on his face. His words are dirty and sexy, and hot as hell, and I get the impression he doesn't declare his intentions with every conquest. He's already told me this is different and despite my best attempts, I want to believe I'm different to him.

He lunges forward, capturing my hands and pinning me back to the bed.

"Don't close your eyes. I want to watch you. I want you to watch me," he growls. My eyes peek open, and I'm rewarded with his sexy as sin smile. He starts in earnest with his bewitching kisses. His tongue sweeps gently against mine, and I don't try to hide my moan. I press my thighs together because the ache is becoming distracting.

He moves down my neck, planting more kisses as he goes before he slips my knickers over my hips. My body tenses for a moment until he kisses the crease of my thigh and I start hoping he'll continue to kiss and lick my pussy. The teasing torment he's lavishing on me fires up a storm of lust, desperate to break free. But he won't be rushed. He's taking his time, and it's killing me.

I spread my legs wide in welcome as he settles between them. Finally, after what seems like hours, his tongue licks at my pussy so softly, it tickles more than excites. The hum of satisfaction rumbling from his chest only makes me want him more. His hands grip my thighs as he kisses and licks and forces my pussy open. He laps at my desire and thrusts his tongue deep inside of me.

"Oh, fuck… Jake!" Pleasure spirals through my body and my head rolls back as my eyes close again. My pleasure twists inside, threatening to take over but I don't want to come yet. I don't want this to be over.

Jake works his tongue inside of me over and over again, careful not to brush my clit. That's all it would take for me to fly. My mumbled cries of delight become a nonsensical stream of words. As if he can feel my climax building, Jake moves his hands and pulls my hips closer so he can seal his lips around my core.

"Yes… yes, please…"

He licks over my clit and flicks the swollen nub as my orgasm peaks. He doesn't stop until I feel the shakes of my limbs subside.

"Ummm, you taste so fucking sweet."

The bed dips as he moves about, but I don't care what he's doing. My eyes remain closed as I bask in the glow of an incredible orgasm. I feel him moving again before he swipes at my weeping core with the head of his cock. Electric sparks bolt through my body, and I jump from my relaxed slumber.

"Time for the main event, baby. Keep your eyes on me." He sweeps his cock through my folds and presses at my entrance before pushing in hard. We both cry out as he slides as deep as he can. My arms come up and wrap around his neck, but I can't look him in the eye. I pull him towards me, and he bites on my throat as he pulls out and thrusts back in.

"Open. Look at me." His hot breath tickles the side of my face, and he rests his forehead against mine. I shake my head and pull my legs around him, pressing him harder against me.

"Fuck, Lily!" He pumps furiously before slowing to a lazy

grind. His teeth nip along my collar bone and around my neck like my personal love necklace. "Stop hiding from me." He pulls back and stares down at me.

Raw passion blazes back at me, and I feel alive. I know how dangerous he is. He woke me up, and he's not stopping there. He's building something between us that's more than just sex, more than just a past fantasy. He's breathing life back into me, and it's terrifying.

I hold his gaze as my desire builds. He stares down as he makes love to me, because that is what this is. He's not fucking me like he did those first times. Jake's showing me something more, and the thought that Jake could feel something real for me hurts as much as it pleasures.

Jake moves his hand and tangles it in my hair, anchoring me to him. I close my eyes, gasping to gain a breath.

"Look at me. Watch me. Feel us. Do it!"

My eyes fly open, and this time, they stay that way.

Jake rocks into me, wrapping the coils of my release tighter and tighter around me until I can't contain it any longer. He thrusts, tipping me over and he follows with a guttural cry as my body contracts around him.

He made me watch—to stay connected to him—while he made love to me and now I'm not sure if it helped my broken heart or just made everything worse.

JAKE

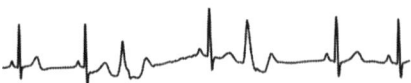

*I*t's amazing how good a night's sleep can feel after missing it for so long. I finally got to sleep without being haunted, because Lily lies next to me. No fight to leave, no argument. And now she's curled up on her side, still asleep in my bed.

For the first time, I can watch her and not feel guilty about it, or hate myself for what I want. She's fucking perfect, and she's back in my life. I don't deserve her, but I don't give a fuck. There was no way I am letting her go again. She is mine. Her leg stretches out under the covers, and she rolls towards me. Her hair is a tangled mess and her dark lashes fan out against the pale of her skin. Visions of her flushed cheeks and bruised lips race in my mind, and I bite back a groan as my dick wakes up at the thought of Lily and what we did last night.

"Morning."

Her breathing has sped up. She's awake.

"Morning."

Her eyes stay closed, and she turns away onto her side again. I don't want her turning away. I want her to turn toward me. God, when did I let her get to me so much? When had I not?

I pull back the covers and head to the shower. A shower is the last thing I want, but I refuse to let her see how much her holding back pisses me off.

The heat from the water wakes me up and settles my nerves. Last night was still vivid, and so was the connection. I feel it, all the way to my core. Getting Lily to see what's between us and admit that we're more than just a convenient hook up will be a lot harder.

I shut off the shower and head out to dress. Lily hasn't moved. She's curled up on her side in my bed. *Where she should be every fucking morning.* I let her be and head to the kitchen.

She joins me about twenty minutes later. Her movements are slow and sleepy. Cautious. Like she's testing something out and not sure how she or I will react. I drink my coffee.

"Would you like a drink?"

"Sure. Coffee please."

I hear her pull a chair out and take a seat at the table. I grab a mug from the cupboard, put the pod into the machine and wait for it to do its thing. She's watching me. I don't even have to turn around to know. The familiar hum that sets all my nerves alight vibrates through me as soon as my back is turned.

"You used to do that, you know." I turn around to look at her.

"What? I'm not doing anything." Her face scrunches up in confusion. I hand her the hot coffee and take my place standing against the counter.

"You used to watch me. When you thought I wasn't looking."

"I didn't. You're clearly imagining it or got me muddled with all the other girls who were after you." She clings to her mug and avoids my eyes.

"You did. I don't think anyone noticed apart from me."

She gets up from the table and heads to the sink and pours half her drink away. The clink of her cup against the marble counter-top cracks in the air.

"You barely noticed me, Jake." She shakes her head and a curtain of brown shields her face from me.

This is more like the Lily I used to know. Not the feisty ice queen I first met at the club. "Listen to me." I move to stand in front of her and force her to look at me. My fingers grip her jaw and give her no choice. "Look at me. Look. You drove me fucking crazy. I wanted you, but I couldn't have you."

"Why?" She makes it sound like a plea.

"Because you were you. You were innocent and pure. You were the good, the only good in my life and I couldn't contaminate you. You were the living evidence that life didn't have to be complete shit. I didn't want to corrupt you."

"You were a complete bastard to me even if you were trying to protect me. You still hurt me."

"If I had treated you the way I wanted to, the way I *still* want to…" I stare into her blue eyes, still dark and stormy from heartache.

"I wouldn't have broken. I would have taken what you gave. We managed being friends." She shuts her eyes and breaks our connection. "I can't think about it now."

"You can't keep trying to push your memories away. Or your feelings. It's not doing you any good."

"Really? You think I don't know that?" She breaks free of my hold and paces to the other side of the kitchen. "I've been pretty good at locking things away until you showed up and sent everything to shit." She pulls her arms around herself, physically holding herself up. She's struggling. She's finally yielded to me, but that alone isn't going to be enough to banish her ghosts.

"Okay, forget the past. What about now? I'm pretty sure we have zero chance of keeping our friendship out of the bedroom. And just so you're crystal clear, I don't want that. If last night isn't enough to prove it to you…"

"Stop! Can't you see I'm not ready? Can't you see what this is doing to me?" Her eyes shimmer as tears form and threaten to fall. Watching as she crumbles ravages me. Her tears finally trail down her cheeks. I want this woman so much, want to be with her on such a primal level that I feel her pain as acutely as if someone punched me in the gut.

I cradle her shuddering body against mine. Lily cries harder, her body shaking in my arms and a wave of possession washes through me. I've never allowed myself to be close to anyone, but I want to feel close to Lily. Anger, hurt and aggression all swarm in my stomach, desperate to lash out.

I have no clue what to say or how I should act, so I continue to hold her and offer her all the comfort of my body until she calms in my arms. She feels good pressed against me, as if she belongs here. My arms hold her tighter, and I breathe her in, enjoying this moment where she lets me be close and doesn't fight it.

I thought I'd reached her last night when I forced her focus on me; when I maintained eye contact as I buried myself deep inside her. Sex with Lily was the closest I'd ever come to making love. There was a moment where she gave in and let the intensity of being together mean something to her. It sure as hell meant something to me. I didn't quite know exactly what, but I was going to be there for her.

"You feel any better for that?" I run my hand up and down her back.

"Yes, thank you." Her face is paler than usual, contrasting harshly with the red blotches and puffy eyes. I would be more than happy to see her like this as a result of a night of unchecked sex—Lily living out my every fucking fantasy—but not like this. "I need to leave." She turns around and dusts herself off, running her hands down the front of her top and jeans.

"Why?" I didn't mean for it to come out as a growl.

"Because, I need to. I need to think about a few things."

"Think about them here. I don't want you running away from me. Ever since I saw you again, you've been running."

"The only time in my life I haven't wanted you to chase me, you have. I'm sorry about last night. I thought we could be friends.

I wanted to, but we can't."

"No. You don't get to choose that."

"Yes, I can. We fucked... that's it."

Her continued dismissal is pissing me off. My hand slams down on the counter making her jump.

"No. You don't get to put last night down as another fuck. I saw it, I felt it. It was more than just a quick fuck. And I'm fucking tired of having the same argument with you over this. Why are you running now? And don't lie to me Lily."

"Because it *did* mean something." Her voice rings with accusation.

"Finally. But I don't understand why you still want to run?"

"Because..."

"Tell me."

"I can't." She turns away from me. Her head drops and her hair slides around her shoulders, concealing her further.

"Have you ever talked about the accident or losing Tim?"

"No. And I'm not about to now."

Her voice is so small. I can only imagine how much it cost her to admit that.

"I think you need to. We finally have a chance and I don't want you running because of the past. It is just that, Lily. In the past. And you better start understanding I want to be a big fucking part of your future."

Right then I know Lily is as damaged as I am. We might not have been right for each other all those years ago, but there is nothing standing in our way now.

16
LILY

Heartache ripped through my chest. Again. How could a teenage love mean so much to me? How can he mean so much, still, despite everything? I can't feel like this. I am falling back in love with the boy who stole my heart so many years ago. Did I ever get it back from him? My stomach drops and churns violently at the thought that perhaps I never stopped loving him.

Everything Jake is saying is what I've longed to hear, that a part of me needs to hear. He is still everything he was at school, just magnified. He is rough and harsh and passionate. But I know that's just a part of him. I've seen a softer side of him. Moments, like last night, and just now, they prove to me what I've always known. He cares for me.

"Hold me?" I need Jake. He is right. I have to stop running. I'd been doing it a very long time.

Strength encompasses me as I'm turned and pulled against Jake's chest. I love this man, but admitting it hurts. "Whatever I do, there's pain. I can't escape from it. I've grown numb, but you make me feel. The good and the bad. I can't take any more of the bad, Jake. I need something good in my life, and I'm scared what that will mean if you're the hope I need." I choke on a sob that bubbles up from my chest. "You don't have a good track record for sticking around."

"You've always been the good in my world. You were a ray of

hope for me. You fought for us. You always did even though I was an arsehole. It wasn't our time, Lily. But it can be now. I promise we can work through this together."

"You don't know who I am anymore. I keep telling you I'm not the same, and you don't listen." I mumble into his t-shirt. Talking without any eye contact like this is easier. I don't feel so exposed to him.

"I know everything I need to."

I don't challenge him and let the time fade away.

"I don't want you to run, Lily. Come on. Come back to bed. Let me just… help you."

He starts moving us to the bedroom, and I don't fight it. He sits down on the bed and shuffles back, propping himself up against the headboard. His arms open wide and I gladly crawl into them, feeling the strength and relief that come from being wrapped up by him.

More time passes with nothing but the gentle rise and fall of his chest to mark it. I push all my woes from my mind and try to focus on what I'm feeling towards this man, my oldest friend who I loved, once upon a time. Was it love I felt now?

"Will you tell me about it?"

"Huh? What?"

"What happened to you?"

Jake's question freezes me in place. I'd been running from this for such a long time I wasn't sure if I'd be capable of telling the story.

"Why?"

"I think we both need it. I told you I want to be in your future. I don't want the past to come between us. But I also need to understand what happened."

I keep my place snuggled against his chest. It had been a long time since I felt close enough to anyone to be able to talk.

"It was raining. It had been raining for days. We'd been away to Wales for the weekend but the weather was awful, so we came back a little early. Tim was driving, and we'd just joined the motorway—the final leg of the journey. We were nearly home.

"There was a crash. I can't remember what happened leading up to it. I do remember feeling jolted, being tossed around inside the car. Pain. It was so hot. It flared through me. My hip, thigh and stomach all hurt to the point of nausea. I thought I was going to pass out. The car stopped moving, but it was still raining. I could see the rain landing on the windscreen, but it was also landing on my face.

"I looked over at Tim, but he wasn't moving. The side of the car was crushed in towards his chest. There was something sticking out his sternum. Out of his chest. Blood dripped down and mixed with the rain, turning everything red. He was so pale, his face..." I swallow and take a few breaths as the vivid memory projects the scene in front of me.

"I could smell rust in the air, that tangy, acrid smell. I didn't know what it was to start with but realised it was blood. Tim's blood. And mine. I looked down and saw my side of the car was crumpled in around my legs. I couldn't move. I tried to, but a mind melting pain ripped through me. I could breathe, I was conscious, so I turned to Tim. He was so pale. He wouldn't answer me when I called. He didn't move or respond when I grabbed him. The pool of blood surrounding him got bigger and bigger, and there was nothing I could do to help him."

"There were noises, stuff happening outside of the car, but it was just a blur. I watched Tim die in front of me. He bled out in front of me, and there was nothing I could do. I couldn't move. I couldn't scream. I couldn't help him."

"My pelvis was crushed. The surgeon said it was a complete

disruption, rotationally and vertically unstable. I didn't know what that meant. They rushed me to surgery. Due to blood loss, I almost died, and there were… complications." I pause. I couldn't deal with this revelation—not yet. "I was in the hospital for months. I lay there hooked up to tubes and relived watching the man I loved die in front of my eyes. The accident left me with nothing but physical pain and memories. I didn't want to live for a while. I think a piece of me died with Tim." I halt my rambling and close my eyes. I feel drained just talking about this. There was much more I could say. About Mum and Dad trying to get me to talk to them or someone. About how I cut myself off from my friends. How Charlotte stopped visiting because I pushed her away. How I didn't have the courage to say goodbye to any of them and just packed up and left. Horrible things happened to me, yet it's only now that I can feel it. I wanted to shove everything away after the accident. I was done with caring. What good had it done? I had always played by life's rules, and I still lost. What more could happen to me? The bitterness inside of me festered and I let it win. Until Jake walked back into my life.

Despite the sadness that threatened to take over, it is a relief to reveal some of the burdens I've carried. I can see what I had done and why. Finally, I could see the events as what they were and not just what had been done to me. Perhaps now I can be free to forgive that woman and create a new Lily.

Jake doesn't say anything for a long while. I don't know if he is waiting for me to say more, but for now, I am done. *Baby steps.*

JAKE

I am a superficial, arrogant bastard who doesn't deserve the good fortune to possess the girl right in front of me. Listening to Lily talk about the accident causes me physical pain. I haven't known loss or hurt—not in the way Lily described. Rage and fury rears up within me and takes over. I have a dark nature in contrast to Lily. But pain isn't something familiar to me. I usually cause it, not experience it. Although when it came to Lily, I'd do anything to prevent causing her pain. Even when I was a kid, not dragging Lily into my world had been a priority. It's what fuelled my internal battles for so many years. I wasn't perfect, and my frustrations got the better of me on occasion, but not anymore.

I take a ragged breath at the thought of losing her like she lost Tim. The urge to squeeze her and not let her go is unbearable, and my arms hold her tighter against me. Now she is here I don't want to let her go. I am done being the bastard I know I have been to her. It might have taken a shitload of time and heartache to reach this point, but I don't want to be that person with Lily now. She's been through enough, and now it is my turn to step up for her.

"Are you going to say anything?" she whispers, but the strain in her voice booms in my ears.

"Not yet." My voice is a little wobbly. I wasn't one for emotion. "We can't stay like this."

"Why not?"

"Because I feel raw and open. Being like this with you makes it worse. I need something to take my mind off of all the bad things."

I take another deep breath and my mind immediately grabs the one thing that will be sure to clear both our heads. Sex. Sex with Lily is off the fucking charts. As much as making love to her felt good, I don't want good. I want the passionate, earth-shattering, never-want-it-to-end sex that I know we're just as good at.

"I can think of a few things." I roll my hips suggestively and she eyes me with a sideways glance.

"I need to go for a swim. It's the only sensible way for me to block everything out. It works for me."

"Swim?" I ask as she pushes herself up off of my chest. Her face remains blotchy and sad dissolving any thought of sex.

"Yes, swim." She smiles, knowing full well where my mind had gone.

She scoots from the bed and heads out to the kitchen. "I'll stop at home to grab my things and then I'm off to the pool."

"What about later?" The question is out before I even engage my brain. She just looks at me with a question all over her face. "Will you be coming back?"

"Here? Probably not today."

"Don't you think we should talk? About us?" *Fuck!* I sounded like all of those women I've shoved out my door. She smiles at me but doesn't answer. I wrestle with myself and sit down at the small kitchen table. She closes the door as she leaves. My head falls into my hands. Not even twenty-four hours with this girl and I was done for.

This girl, this woman, is the most important thing in my life. The Lily from our school days was the light to my darkness. I want her eyes to shine with a brilliance that is impossible not to notice. I want her to have strength and happiness, and I have a pretty good idea of how I'm going to give that to her. *Maybe I'm not such a bastard.*

LILY

*A*ll the laps in the world can't help me today.

Jake is at the forefront of my mind, together with Tim and how I've abandoned life since his death. I don't want to dwell on the past. I've done enough looking back. I have other things to occupy my mind now.

I stop when my fingers touch the wall and let my breathing calm down. The water laps around me, gently supporting me. Jake is right. We do need to talk about us. The last twenty-four hours have been an emotional downpour. Good and bad. At least things were more open between us. I don't have to hide behind my behaviour. He knows, now, why I wasn't the same person I used to be and what I had lost.

I can't help the sliver of hope that maybe my past won't make a difference in how he sees me, and he will love the damaged girl inside of me.

After my swim, I eat a light dinner, take a shower and fall into bed, the exhaustion from the weekend finally catching up with me.

I haven't contacted Jake, but I will. We'd been fighting the tie between us for years. Finally, for whatever reason, we have a second chance. I have a second chance, and I'm not stupid enough to turn it down. I'm right back to where I'd been as a girl, and the love I use to feel for him demanded acknowledgement...and action. I pick up my phone.

> *Hey. A lot's happened this weekend. I have work this week, but perhaps we could meet up to talk. You're right.*

We do need to talk about us. Lily

Good. I'm not happy about waiting to talk though. Why can't we talk right now?

Really? I won't run, but I don't want to rush this. Lily

Rush? We've been skirting around this for years and I don't want to have this conversation over the fucking phone.

OMG calm down.

Jake had always had a temper. You knew his emotions seethed, ready to blow, barely held in check under the surface. His potential for volatile behaviour was one of the aspects of his nature that fascinated me, but then, I'd never witnessed him physically explode. Around me, he'd been stoic. The first few times we'd had sex were the closest I'd ever come to being on the receiving end of his unchecked emotion. Talk about wicked. I lit the fuse and benefited from the explosion between us.

My phone vibrates in my hand, and I glance at the screen. Jake.

"Hi," I answer.

"I'm outside and want you to let me up. I'll be two minutes."

"What?"

He hangs up before I can question him.

I pull myself from my bed and go and open the front door. I leave it on the latch. If he's in such a hurry to see me, he will have to put up with me being an exhausted mess. A couple of minutes later his heavy footfalls sound through the house.

"Why was your door open?"

Not the first question I thought he'd lead with. "Because you said you were coming up." I'm curled on the bed where I want to be.

"You shouldn't leave the door open like that. Anyone could have walked in."

"It's no big deal, Jake. You said you'd only be a minute."

"Fine. I didn't come here to argue." He takes a couple of steps and sits at the end of the bed. "I want us to talk, and I want it to be face to face. I don't want to wait for a few days, and I don't ever want you to forget what we shared last night. I meant what I said. I intend to be a part of your future, and that means there will be an us. You might not feel like you're ready, but I am. I've just got you back. I'm not risking that for the world."

O*h, my!*

"So, when you said you wanted to talk, you meant you were going to tell me how this is going to work?"

"Remember all of those texts you sent me. All the times you wanted to meet for coffee or pushed for some sort of catch up? Well, I fought them. But you wouldn't let our friendship go. For some reason, you saw something in me that made you work for us. Everything was screaming at me just to take you, and fuck you out of my system and never look back. But I knew I'd regret it for the rest of my life. I'd been that guy to countless women. They were all happy to have what I was putting out if it meant they got a piece of me. You quietly got on with your life while I kept a safe distance, but you pushed and pushed and wouldn't let me go. You were the only one, Lily. You were the good. You were the innocent, and by staying away from you, I saved a piece of my soul. For you.

"You wouldn't take no from me. Now it's my turn to return that favour. I'm not going to take no for an answer. It might hurt, but I know we can make the pain go away. I want to stop you from aching, baby. God, I'd do anything to help you, and I don't want to be apart from you. I want us together, as of right fucking now."

He moves off the bed and kneels at the side, making sure he's right there in my line of sight. He strokes my hair from my face, and smiles.

That smile...some last, wounded piece of me surrenders. I've lost the desire to resist him. I lean up on my elbow and close the distance between us. I defy any woman not to melt into this man after that not so little speech. It is one of those moments where the world spins and realigns in the blink of an eye and now all I can see, all I can think of, is Jake.

My lips trace his before I deepen the kiss. He takes over and straddles me, pushing me back into the mattress. His lips tease, and the sweep of his tongue against mine ignites my nerves. I want him to take it further, to push and pull and send my body into orbit, but he doesn't. He holds back. His hands keep me grounded. He ravishes me with his gentleness. He's showing me how much he cares, and he's breaking my heart all over again.

I pull away, not able to take any more tenderness. My jaw clenches and I fight the onslaught of tears. "Jake, I just… just hold me."

He rolls to the side and stretches his arm for me to cuddle into.

"Thank you."

"You're welcome, baby."

LILY

*I*t was a surreal week. After being on my own and only looking out for me, it was novel to have someone to talk to in the evening, to share a conversation with. Jake demanded a key to my apartment on Monday morning, and I couldn't find a reason to fight him.

Jake didn't want us spending time apart outside of work, even at night. But as our friendship rekindled, so did the doubts I still harboured. I hadn't told him what all of my scars were from. That was for a later time, but I felt self-conscious around him. I wasn't the confident, sassy woman anymore. She had existed because I'd used random sex to smother my emotions. I hadn't cared what I did as long as I didn't have to feel.

Jake made me care. I cared what he thought of me as a woman, and I didn't want him to see my imperfect and ugly body. I hid my scars because I hated them. Every time I looked at them, I saw the raised, welted skin and misshapen muscles as an outward indication of the internal devastation, both to my body and to my soul. My anxiety builds. I need to tell him.

Jake interrupts my introspection. "Do you want to go out tonight?"

"Another date?" I'm not sure I could take another trip to the cinema.

"I promise, no films. Just a meal. I'm usually home late from work and don't worry about food too much. We can stay at mine tonight. I'm looking forward to sleeping in tomorrow."

"Dinner sounds fine, but nothing fancy. I'll go and change."

Twenty minutes later we walk out of the building and head to a little bistro about ten minutes from home. Both our neighbourhoods brimmed with a diverse range of cafés, restaurants and shops, all benefitting from the hustle and bustle of being so close to the centre of London.

The quaint restaurant Jake chose has several long wooden benches as opposed to individual tables. The menu is scrawled on a chalkboard and has half a dozen starter and main courses listed. It is a take on tapas—ordering several dishes from what was on offer to share.

We arrived early, but the place was crowded with only a few spaces left. The waitress indicates for us to grab the last two spots at the end of the furthest table and we wait for her to take our drink order.

"What do you fancy?" I ask.

"Something meaty. The BBQ ribs and the corn sound good and maybe the salad?" Jake rattles off his choices which sound great. I add a bruschetta to the list, and we order straight away.

"You mentioned you usually work late. You've been home shortly after me all week. Is that going to change?" I ask, realising Jake might have been trying to keep a closer eye on me than I first thought.

"Probably. But you'll be living with me soon so it won't matter so much." He grins, showing me all of his perfectly white teeth as if he just cracked a joke.

"Excuse me?"

"Well, I'm sure the rent on your place is a fortune. Property around here is ridiculous."

"Who said I pay rent?"

He gives me a quizzical look.

"So, you have a staggering mortgage to pay on the place?"

"No." I enjoy watching him struggle through this conversation.

"Lily, it's little more than a glorified shoe box, but it would have cost a small fortune. Like hundreds of thousands of pounds."

"Are you done second guessing me?"

He shrugs, giving me the floor.

"Tim had life insurance. That and the sale of the house in Bristol meant I could buy it when it came on the market. How much are you spending on your place? It's much bigger than mine."

"Too much. I'm sorry I assumed."

"It's alright." The waitress brings us our drinks, and we allow the hubbub of the place to drown out the lingering tension from our conversation. Despite Jake being one of my oldest friends, we barely know each other.

A few minutes later, the food arrives, and we both take a share from the large plates and enjoy the tasty morsels. Conversation is non-existent, and although we'd sat through periods of silence in the past, this feels different. Harder, somehow.

We finish the food and Jake stands and heads to the counter to pay.

He takes my hand in his as we leave the restaurant and he starts us back towards home.

"I want you to move in. I thought it would be an obvious choice as you could stop paying rent. You owning the place threw me a bit. It doesn't change that I want to be with you, though."

"Don't you think moving in is a little sudden? We've spent one week together. That's not a basis to live together." He's lost his fucking mind.

"Perhaps, but it would be a lot easier than you coming to my place or vice-versa each evening."

"I'm pleased we're working at being a couple, but this is ridiculous. Have you even lived with anyone before?"

"I don't see how that's relevant. Just because I've not done it before doesn't mean I don't want it now."

"You might think you do, but please, you've sprung a fucking ton of stuff on me since last week. This is a step too far."

"How else am I going to get you to open up to me?"

"What do you mean? I have opened up to you."

"No, babe...you keep me out. You're lost in your thoughts half the time. I come to see you, and you're sitting in that chair, staring at nothing, miles away. I want to make you feel better, Lily, and I have no fucking clue how to do that at the moment. I told you how I feel, how I've always felt about you. It doesn't seem to have made an impression."

"Knowing how you feel means a huge amount. You have no idea. But please, it's only been a few days. You've done a huge amount to help me already. Don't get impatient. You said you want me in your future, well that's a long fucking time, so don't rush it."

We enter my building and head up in silence.

"I won't push the house thing tonight *if* you agree to go someplace with me next weekend."

"Are you going to tell me where you want to take me?"

"No. Deal or no deal, baby?" He kisses me shorting out my answer.

"Yes," I groan. God, my feet have barely touched the ground this week, and he's still springing things on me. He reminds me of a child in some respects. He wants everything now.

JAKE

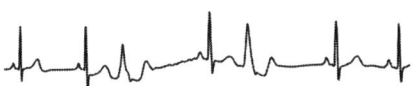

I'm pretty sure I'm cocking up on the friend and boyfriend front. I'd refused any physical space between us over the last few weeks, but I can feel something is missing, but I have no fucking idea what. All I know is I want to find it and fix it.

My grand gesture about living together crashed and burned in spectacular fashion. My reasoning as to why it would be logical held no water if she didn't need to financially. But, she doesn't understand. I've waited for far too fucking long to be with her. I don't want to wait one second more.

After this weekend, we might not be speaking again. We'll see. It would involve a little white lie and a mountain of forgiveness, but I know it is needed. This is what Lily needs, and that's what my goal is. To give her what she needs.

"Are you ready to go? You just need a small overnight bag. Nothing fancy."

"Yes, although it would be a lot easier if you just told me what we were doing."

"That would spoil the surprise and the deal we had, remember."

"Alright."

We make it down to the Audi, and I load the bags in the back of the car. A pang of guilt washes over me at what I'm doing, although I know it's the right thing, part of me wants to give her some warning.

It takes a good couple of hours to get out of London and onto the M4.

"I know you said this was a surprise, Jake, but I'd like to know now."

The M4 is the direct route towards Bristol, and although there are plenty of places we could be going, her instincts are firing.

"We're going to see my family. Andy and his wife are expecting. I was due to head home this weekend, and I didn't want to leave you." The lie trips off my tongue but wraps around my chest like barbed wire.

"Your family?" The lift in her voice is impossible not to notice. She was always interested in them. She'd met Andy a handful of times, but I kept her away from my parents. She didn't really ask about them, although I knew she wanted to. We avoided the subject as our own unwritten rule. I knew she'd be interested, and that was why I told her this is what we'd be doing. She settles back in her seat, and I continue to cruise along the motorway.

The closer we get, the more my gut clenches with apprehension. This could backfire spectacularly, but I remember the look on her parents faces when I visited.

"Jake, where do your parents live?"

"Not far now."

"If you're doing what I think you might, you better get ready to turn around and head home."

"And what might that be?"

"Taking me to see *my* parents."

"Why would I do that?"

"I don't know, but at the moment I wouldn't put it past you. You've been trying to mend me ever since you locked me in your fucking house."

She rages at me, but I keep on course.

"Seriously, Jake. You can't make me do this. I'm not ready. This isn't something you can fix for me."

My tact is to ignore her. She can't physically throw herself out of the car, and she can't stop me from where I'm driving. I'll deal with the consequences later, but she's right. I am trying to fix her, or at least help her to move on with her life so there's a future for us.

"Jake, please don't make me do this. I beg you. If you care for me, if you want to make things work between us then give me some time. I'm not ready. Stop… turn around!"

Each volley of pleas hit me harder and harder. I said I didn't want to hurt her anymore, and right now I was. God, I said I'd be better for her. Was this a mistake?

I park the car and turn tentatively towards Lily. She's staring out the window at her house. I reach for the hand in her lap, but she snatches it away.

"They want to see you. They want to know you're alright."

"How could you possibly know that. You have no right, Jake. You can't do this, you've fucked up this time…"

"I know because I came to see them after you went AWOL on me." I let that bit of information sink in before I continue. "I told you. You aren't going to slip through my fingers, but I had no idea where you lived. So, I came back here. I saw Charlotte and your parents."

Her eyes mist as she listens.

"They miss you, baby. They just want to know you're safe. Please. You've come so far in the last few weeks. You've let me in, and you've opened up. I want this to help you. You need to make peace with this as well as what happened to Tim."

Tears trace the contours of her face as she looks at me in sheer and utter panic.

"I can't do this without you, Jake. I can't look them in the eye after everything I've done."

"I'll be right there, baby. Each step of the way."

"Oh god. I've been horrible to them. What do I say?" She lunges across the car, and I hold her while she lets the emotions run through her. If we have to wait in the fucking car for the rest of the day, so be it.

"Tell me when you're ready, and we will do this together. Remember, baby. No more on your own, understand." I kiss the top of her hair and rub circles on her back and hope that she's as strong as I think she is. *Maybe I wasn't such a bastard.*

LILY

*I*f I didn't love him, I'd kill him. How can he do this to me? I stare out the windscreen towards my childhood home. My heart hammers against my chest and beats loudly in my ears.

I'd often thought about coming back and seeing my parents. Every time I wanted to, pain and sorrow shut me down. I'd done so much damage to myself. I'd convinced myself it would be better just to stay away.

The air in the car stifles me, but I can't get out. If I do, I'll have taken the first step towards seeing them again. I deserve the discomfort I'm feeling. I've coped with far worse.

I look around the street where I grew up and struggle to resist the warmth of the memories that naturally come back when I think about my childhood. I had a wonderful childhood. I had great parents and friends. I enjoyed school. I wanted for nothing in the grand scheme of things.

As my mind recalls the joyful and fulfilled times, it fast-forwards to the tragedy and bitter anger courses up from my gut as I struggle to comprehend the sheer loss from that day. Tim lost his life. Devoted parents lost a cherished son. I lost my friend, my lover, my life-partner, and any future of holding our child in my arms.

"I shouldn't have brought you here without asking you. I wanted to take the first step for you, so you didn't have to." Jake turns the key and the ignition fires.

"No!" My voice cracks with emotion. I turn in my seat and

gaze at Jake. "I need to do this. You're right." Jake is right. He *has* given me the first step. He gifted that to me, and now I need to be the daughter who'd spent many happy years here and not the twisted and angry woman with tears running down her face.

I swipe the tears away and look at Jake.

My hand reaches for the door, and I climb out of the car. I stand frozen in place, paralysed with shame and fear that after all of this time my parents won't understand my crazy behaviour. Jake's hand circles on my back and he gently presses the base of my spine, encouraging me to take the next step forward. My feet stutter but begin moving towards the house. His hand finds mine, and he squeezes it so tight, all of my focus is on the heat and pressure throbbing in my palm.

We walk the few meters to the drive and my shaky hand reaches up to press the doorbell. If Jake weren't holding my hand, I would have run away. There might be a part of me that wants to show a determination to put the past behind me, put it to rest, but at this moment, it's a very small part—a tiny fraction of me, the size of the hand being held in Jake's.

As the seconds pass, the weight of apprehension squeezes my chest, and then Dad opens the door. I watch confusion spread across his face before realisation dawns and his eyes shimmer with joyful tears. It's almost too much. He was never an affectionate father. He did everything I ever asked of him, but I can't remember the last time he gave me a hug. Seeing him like this is enough to make me hate myself and my actions all the more.

"Lily?"

I can't reply. The burn in my throat as the tears build in strength is too much and opening my lips will let out a mass of withheld emotion. I nod and press my lips together tighter. Jake rescues me from having to respond.

"May we come in Mr. Hill?"

Dad reluctantly swings his gaze to Jake, and he opens the door a little wider. I bolt pass my dad and seek refuge in the living room. It's my turn to squeeze Jake's hand, constricting my hand around his as tightly as I can to emphasise how much I'm struggling.

I turn and stare at the door to the hall and expect to see my dad following after, but he doesn't. His absence sends my nerves screaming around my body as if they're a warning system to protect me from any more pain.

"Lily! Lily?"

I hear the distressed cries from my mum and realise he went to fetch her. She rushes into the room and stops dead a few feet away from me. She's in shock. I see it etched into her face. Dad is behind her and rests his hands on her shoulders, providing her the physical comfort and reassurance that Jake offers me.

We all stand motionless for a moment. The little girl trapped inside of me wants to run to my mummy, but I feel there is too much to wade through before we get to that. I take a step back and pull Jake down onto the sofa with me. I perch on the edge and nod to the two chairs opposite.

We're all walking on egg shells, but we're in the same room. This morning, speaking to my parents, hell, *seeing* my parents was a million miles away from anything I thought could happen.

"Are you okay, Lily? You look good." Mum breaks the silence.

"Yes. Yes, I'm fine. Mum, this is Jake. Dad, I think you've already met him." I push the words past my trembling lips.

"Hello, Mrs. Hill." Jake steps forward to greet my mum.

"Are you staying? Would you like a drink? I can make tea?" Mum busies herself. Watching her so upset and visibly hurting breaks my heart even more. The pain in my past has mellowed. It doesn't have the sharp edges that used to bite deep and hard into my soul. Watching my parents labour with this impromptu reunion is crippling. She doesn't wait for me to say anything, just retreats from the room. I cling to Jake's hand even harder as I weigh what I should do. The daughter I was would go and see if she's alright. I want to do that, at least a part of me does, but I'm terrified of what might happen if she's as torn-up by this as I am. I've not spoken to my mum in years. Can I still go up to her and give her a hug? Will she accept me?

I spring after her. She's bent over the kitchen sink, her hand cupping her mouth as she cries to herself.

"Mum... I'm... sorry..." I start, but I sob it out in great big barks of tears as my body shudders. I clear the distance and wrap my arms around her. She engulfs me with hers, and our tears dampen our cheeks and shoulders. I clutch her close and try to physically impress all the words I'm incapable of saying. We stay like this for a while. It's as if neither of us wants to let go in case we break this moment and never get it back. My decision to isolate myself has had wider consequences than just its effect on me. If not for Jake, I would have let my dysfunction continue.

I snuggle closer into my mum's embrace and let her presence soothe a part of me. She didn't push me away. She didn't reject me. We might not have said one word to each other, but we're taking a step forward.

My eyes sting as I try and blink a few times. My eyes feel as if I've been crying for weeks—inflamed and angry, painful no matter what I do.

I hear the bass of voices talking in the other room. Jake's been alone with my dad for god-knows how long. At least they are talking.

"I better make that tea now," Mum whispers into my neck. I reluctantly pull away and stare at her blotchy face. I nod and head back out to the living room.

"Hi, Dad."

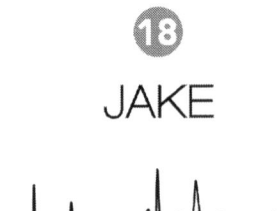

JAKE

*L*istening to Lily cry with her mother is harrowing. Each sob feels like a punch to the stomach. I can't keep still. Neither Mr. Hill nor I can look at one another, let alone talk.

Minutes pass, and the initial distress peters out. All we can hear is the shuddering breaths from the other room and the occasional shuffle from our uncomfortable silence.

"I, err, need to thank you for bringing her home."

I look up, concerned he might think that Lily is here to stay.

"Well, she didn't know about the visit. I took a gamble that it was best for her. She just didn't know how to take the first step."

"Well, I'm grateful it's been made. Perhaps now we can start helping our girl again."

"I'll make sure she doesn't stay away."

"So, are you the new boyfriend? Must admit, didn't think I'd see you again after you left a few weeks back."

"I wasn't going to let her slip through my fingers. And yes, I'm the boyfriend." I straighten on the sofa as I say the words.

"You make sure you do right by her. You may have good intentions, but I won't have anyone treating my baby poorly. She's been through enough."

"I want her to lay her ghosts to rest, and I want her sparkle back. I want her to be happy and not just treading water."

"Do you love her?" It was the first time he looked me in the eye.

"Yes. Yes, I do."

"Very well then." He goes back to clenching his fists in his lap.

"Hi, Dad." Lily appears at the door, and I can't stop the smile on my face.

"We're staying in town tonight. Hotel du Vin."

"Okay." Lily hasn't said more than a few words since leaving her folks. Reuniting them had been the right thing to do. Her silence is fraying my nerves. I want to lash out and shake her, make her speak to me, force her to tell me what she is thinking. She sits motionless in the car, her eyes staring out at the passing vehicles and roads.

I turn into the narrow road off of the city centre and park the car. Lily opens the door and walks around to me. I grab the case from the back and take her hand. At least she isn't pushing me away. We check in and go up to the plush bedroom. Lily goes to the leather tub seat in the corner and curls her legs up to her chest. She does this far too often for my liking.

I set the case on the desk and go to retrieve her. I pull her up out of the chair and wrap her in my arms. She's soft and pliant, as if she's almost given up. I can't have that. I sit us back on the king bed and wrap her around me, in every way I can think. It does me a fuck-load of good. I just hope she feels it too.

"Thank you," her lips whisper against my skin. "Thank you for being stronger than I am."

I close my eyes as relief surrounds me. She's talking to me, and her words make me feel so damn good.

"I'll always be strong for you, baby. You don't need to worry about that anymore."

"I've done so many awful things. Embarrassing, degrading, hurtful things."

"And you needed to go through that. It was your way of dealing with tragedy. It's in the past. It's all in the past." I hug her harder to me.

Every fibre of my being screams out for me to claim her, to push away all of her bad memories with my body. Despite the sombre mood, I grit my teeth to avoid rolling my hips into her. With her long legs wrapped around my waist, all that prevents me from sinking deep inside her are several layers of material. My baser instincts will have to wait. I need to show I can comfort her as well as fuck her, although right now, I wish I could do both.

She's not crying. Her cheek rests tightly against my throat like she's burrowed into me, seeking comfort. Her clean, fresh scent surrounds me, intoxicating me.

"I know what you want. I can feel it, the tension in your body, your restraint."

Her admission does little to help my mood and rising arousal. "It doesn't matter, baby."

"It does. You admitted to me that you didn't want to ruin the innocent Lily when we were younger. The only reason we're together now is that you saw me as an easy target to fuck with your friend. I acted the same way with you as I've done with countless men over the last few years. I let you have me the way you wanted. If I was still the innocent girl you remember, none of that would have happened. The only reason we're here now is because of my slutty behaviour. The thought of what I did with all those other men makes me sick... but it led me back to you." She sits up. Her hands cup my jaw, and she runs her fingers through the scrape of several days of stubble. "For you, I'd do it all over again. I wouldn't change the way I acted if it meant we'd be together. That's what you mean to me. I want to keep you in my life."

My lips seek hers, but I hold back. "I don't want the woman I first met at the club. I want the girl who was my best friend. I want the woman who screams my name and gets my blood so fucking hot I want to explode. I want who you were and who you are now, but above everything, I want you happy. I've been waiting for you my whole fucking life. I can't change my tastes and what I enjoy, but I know you enjoyed every fucking thing I did with you. Who says we can't have it all?"

I stand and pick her up. Talking about Lily and what I want has sent all my blood to my dick. Gone is any self-control, not that I ever had much. She holds herself up against me, and my hands palm her arse, all tight and round and a perfect fit for me. My head skips ahead to my cock sunk in her slick heat while she sits on my lap and rides me so fucking hard I must brace against the wall.

The room doesn't allow for my fantasy, so I settle for the chair. I ease Lily away from my body and work my fingers over the clothes keeping her from me. I strip her down to her beautiful skin before taking my clothes off. We stand in front of each other. Every muscle in my body is twitching to touch her. She waits, patiently for me to lead and I fucking love it. For the first time, I can see all of her, a gorgeous expanse of creamy skin for me to master. My eyes skip across the scar on her hip and stomach. I don't care about it. I'm simply so god-damn thankful she's alive. The growl that rumbles in my chest is all about possession.

I attack her lips and crush our bodies together. She's soft under my touch but doesn't pull away. Her tongue licks at mine with the same intensity as always. My hands can't get enough, travelling the length of her spine, tangling in her hair, squeezing the dip at her waist. I want all of her, forever.

Her little gasps as my fingers work across her skin block everything out of my mind. Turning this girl on is addictive. I lift her up, and she clings to my body. This time, when I grab her arse, I get to enjoy the real feel of it in my hands. My fingers dig in, and she tightens her hold on my neck. Our kisses grow demanding and fevered. I sit in the tub chair and slouch back to give her access to my body. She grinds her sweet pussy onto my dick, sending my teeth into her plump bottom lip. We both stare at each other for a few seconds before she moves again, sliding her wet heat over my cock. I let her lips go and block out the impending need to raise her and slam her down onto me.

"This is all for you, baby. I'm right here for you," I murmur.

She lifts up on her forearms and begins a lap-dance of torture. Her tits brush against my chest and up to tempt my tongue, but she rolls back and presses down so I can feel just how hot she is.

I can't control my hands, and I anchor one to her hip while I sit forward to reach around her with the other, seeking out her glistening pussy. I coat my finger with her desire, teasing her as she teases me. Her choked moan is another red flag to my raging hard-on.

"I want to tease you, and I want to drive you crazy… don't… tempt me." Her husky voice is just another thing to add to the long-arse list of things this girl does for me.

"Fuck, you are driving me crazy. I want to shove you down on my dick so badly. I want to hear your moans echo around this room and ring in my ears as I make you come."

"Stop… I want…"

"What do you want? Hmm? I want you to do whatever's in your pretty head. If that's go slow, have gentle, loving sex, then we'll do that. But if you want to ride me so hard you can't breathe because you're so desperate to come, then fucking do it." I see her pupils blacken the blue of her eyes, and I rest my head back on the chair and count in my head. *One, two…*

She grabs the base of my dick and rubs the tip through her pussy lips. A silky warmth charges every atom of my body. My teeth clench as I force my body to remain still. She seats herself in one swift move. She drops her head back, arching her spine and pressing her tits forward. *What the fuck did I do to deserve this?*

My eyes droop as I watch the woman I love fuck me. She undulates and rocks on my lap, and I watch her every breath as she takes her fill of me. Her movements quicken, and I feel the subtle tightening of her pussy as I try not to ram into her. Her fingers dig into my shoulders as she starts to ride me with an abandon I love. She slides up and down my shaft again and again until her quivering is almost too much for me to take. The building heat of my pleasure settles at the base of my spine, ready to explode. The look of abandon she wears undoes me.

"Jake… god… I want to come… I want to come so badly…" She locks her arms and smashes down on my dick, the force almost sending me blind with a need to come.

"Jake… yes! Yes!... Fuck, yes!" She cries out as she finally comes, squeezing me like a fucking vice. I wrap my arms around her body and bite her neck while I ram my hips forward and fuck her until I come. Every muscle in my body spasms as my balls pull up, and my cock jerks inside her. Sensation rips comprehension from me until all I feel is her.

I lick the bite mark on her skin, sweeping any pain away. Her laboured breathing sends hot puffs of air over my chest as she rests her head on my shoulder. I hold her tightly and stand, staggering towards the bed. We fall onto the pristine sheets and stay motionless. I wait for my stampeding heart to calm, but I have a feeling it will be a while.

"Hmm… I have to admit, I like waking up with you." Wrapped around me is Lily's warm body. Somehow, we managed to get under the covers last night, but god knows I don't remember it.

"It's nice to have someone to cosy up to." She lifts her head, and I see the lightness of spirit in her eyes that I'd missed so much. I plant a kiss on the top of her head and rest my eyes. With everything that happened yesterday I had neglected to mention our plans today.

"When are we leaving?" she mumbles.

"A little later on today."

"Are we seeing your family as well?" She's suddenly sitting up with an eager expression on her face.

"Uh, no."

"Why not?" Her nose scrunches up at my quick dismissal.

"Because I try and stay away from them. Besides, it's not like they want to see me." I pull the covers away and pace to the bathroom. I might be a bastard for having double standards, but I wasn't going to get into a fight with Lily about the lesser qualities of my folks compared to hers.

I set the water running in the shower and turn to the bathroom mirror. Lily's gloriously naked figure appears in my peripheral, and I switch my focus solely to her.

"You don't get to do that. You don't get to dictate to me what battles I fight and then run away from yours."

"It's not the same. I've never had what you could call a loving relationship with my family. What happened yesterday was to help you reconnect with a family that loves you. It's not the same." I turn and step into the huge shower and drench my hair under the streaming water.

Ten minutes later I'm wearing a towel around my waist, and I'm back out in the room. Lily sits in the same chair we fucked in last night. Already dressed.

"Going somewhere?" I ask.

"Yes. We're heading back."

"I don't remember saying we were leaving immediately." I grab a clean pair of boxers from my bag and drop the towel.

"You didn't, but if you're not even going to consider seeing you parents and dismiss my suggestion after what you put me through yesterday, then I'd rather go home."

I close my eyes and take a mental check on my temper. I love this girl, and I put her through hell yesterday. I should be able to handle my frustrations.

"I've never had to explain my parents before. It's not a simple relationship. I hardly see them. It's not a big deal. We can talk about it another day. And I told you we were leaving later today. We're meeting someone first." I shove my legs into new jeans and pull out a clean t-shirt but Lily continues to pull her stuff together, not taking a blind bit of notice of me.

"My parents," I shout to get her attention. She jumps and freezes what she is doing, so I continue. "My parents think Andy hung the moon. In their eyes, he can do no wrong, and me? It's as if I don't exist except to disappoint them. He was a cocky git and enjoyed being one. He got whatever he wanted. What you saw that day was just an example of treatment I've received life long. I tried to be the good son, but nothing ever changed. After a while, I didn't care what they thought. I just did as I pleased. As I got older, I set out to be better than Andy. That's the main reason I came to London." I feel exposed enough as it is so I don't mention my borderline obsession with Lily and how it only fuelled my bad behaviour.

"The rift between my family and me is permanent. Nothing specific happened. There isn't anything that I can fix. It's just the way it is.

"Do you want breakfast?" I offer. I want to change the subject and fast. If she needed more of an explanation she'd have to wait because that's all I have. I feel ready to explode. I turn and see a gentler looking Lily.

"Okay. Thank you. It's been a pretty emotional weekend." She closes the gap between us and wraps her arms around me. "I'm feeling fragile right now. My parents, talking about the past and now hearing a fragment of your pain. No more heartache, okay?"

"Agreed."

She snuggles into my chest and I take a deep breath of her citrus scent to calm my nerves. "I know you probably bulldoze through anything and anyone who disagrees with you, and that's what you're used to, but I don't want to fight with you when we come up against things we don't agree on. I want us to be able to talk."

At least she was thinking of us as together.

"How did we go from waking up happy to fighting?" I wanted to go back to fucking bed and start over.

"We're not fighting. I'm just trying to understand you. We might have known one another a long time ago, but we need to get to know each other now. And talking hasn't been our priority. I know you're uncomfortable opening up, so again, thank you for what you shared." She keeps her arms wrapped around me as if the argument won't annoy me as much if she's within touching distance.

I didn't do talking, but maybe with Lily I'd make an exception.

"You need to learn to trust me."

"You don't just magically trust someone, Jake."

She has no fucking clue. I grab her shoulders and push her out of our embrace.

"You did yesterday. You trusted me. I forced you to do something that was a big fucking deal for you yesterday, and you're struggling. Don't pick a fight with me. If you haven't got it yet, I fucking love you and would do pretty much anything for you, but I won't fight with you. Unless we're in bed." I can't stop the wicked grin on my lips as I picture wrestling Lily underneath me before I pin her and take her.

"You love me?"

Her shocked expression isn't what I'd hoped for. I'm not any type of hearts and flowers guy, but shock isn't what I want from my girl. Not about what she means to me. "Yes."

We both stand looking at each other.

"I didn't think you'd ever say those words." Her voice is so soft. I can hear the emotion caught in her throat. "Well, you're the only one, baby. Get used to it." I break our stand-off and clutch her to me. I rest my forehead against hers and cradle her head in my hands. "You drive me fucking crazy, and I have no clue what I'm doing. But I don't like fighting with you. I fight with everyone else. You are my peace."

Her eyes shimmer and my stomach plummets with the thought of more pain for this girl.

"Don't cry. You've done too much of that."

"I'm sorry, I am. I overreacted. These aren't sad tears. They're… pleased tears. I'm working on happy."

"I'll take that. Can we stop fighting then and grab breakfast? We're meeting a friend in a couple of hours."

"A friend?"

"Charlotte."

LILY

*J*ake Stewart loves me.

That's a pretty big deal. I'm sure I dreamt about it once or twice. And now we're waiting to see Charlotte for lunch.

Jake hasn't said much since the hotel. We had a quiet continental breakfast in the dining room before he packed us up and headed into town. I had believed that being in the same town, on the same streets that I walked with Tim would tear me up. It hasn't.

Compared to walking up the path to my parents, walking into the small restaurant in my old neighbourhood wasn't such a hard job, but knowing who waited for me made my stomach sick with nerves. I'd been horrible to her. I'd thrown her out of the hospital the last time I saw her. *I think.*

I sip my ice water and look around the quiet room to see if I missed her coming in. I can't help myself. The ball of nerves twists and churns in my stomach and I can't contain my fidgeting. Thankfully my emotions are a little more stable than earlier this morning. God, I hadn't felt this… much… since the accident. My heart is having a hard time keeping up, but at least I no longer feel denial is my only option.

The door opens and in walks Charlotte. She hasn't changed a bit, apart from the rather large baby-bump she's sporting. She looks around the restaurant, and her face lights up when our eyes meet. Why I ever thought keeping these people out of my life was a better way to go, I have no idea.

Charlotte stops at the edge of the table and looks to Jake and me before I stand up. She doesn't give me an option and pulls me in for a huge hug.

"I can't believe he got you here."

"I'm sorry… I couldn't…"

"Shhh! I don't want to hear it. You're here, and that's something to celebrate."

I pull back before the waterworks start again. I must have cried a years' worth in the last day alone.

The waiter comes over and takes our drinks order.

"Oh, I'll have a decaf latte please, and an orange juice. Are we eating as well? I'd love to see the menu." Charlotte takes everything in her stride, and I envy the sheer joy she radiates. My eyes fall to her baby-bump, and my own heart stops for a few seconds, thinking about that missing piece of me.

I look over at Jake who seems to have resorted to form and is sitting and brooding about something. The sexy frown hasn't moved from his face since we got here. It reminds me of how he was so insular at school, keeping himself to himself. It's still as mysterious as ever, but now I have a better understanding of what's behind the mask. He said he didn't want to fight, but if we love each other, if he loves me, then surely there is going to be some honest truths we have to overcome.

"What about you, Lily?"

"Sorry, what?"

"Drinks, food?" Charlotte asks with a small smile.

"Umm, sure. I'll have a sparkling water. Maybe we can order food in a few minutes?"

"Sure." She chirps, sending the waiter away.

"Thank you for meeting me today. I didn't realise this was the plan until this morning."

"Seriously, I don't care. You're here." She beams at me. Her smile is set perfectly against her sunshine hair. My eyes fall to her bump again, and when I look up, her smile is still in place.

"I'm due in twelve weeks. I guess Jake didn't mention it."

We both look at him, but he's not paying us any attention. He's staring out into the restaurant. I follow his gaze but only see a waitress delivering food to another table.

"Jake!"

He glares at me but hides it quickly, pulling himself up and into the conversation.

"Yes."

"You didn't mention Charlotte was pregnant."

"Umm, sorry. I didn't notice before."

"That's alright. It wasn't like it was a long conversation."

"Are you married? Are you happy?" I ask, desperate to try and shake the feeling of loss festering in my gut. I rub the damaged side of my hip.

"I've been married a few years now. I would have loved to get in touch…"

"No, it's my fault. I cut all ties. Honestly, I didn't know I had the courage to come back after all this time. Jake kidnapped me and took me to see Mum and Dad." The shock on her face is priceless and a giggle bubbles up from my chest.

"Seriously?"

"Yes. He told me when it was pretty obvious where we were heading. I nearly jumped out the car I was so afraid."

Charlotte reaches across the table to still my worrying hands.

"I don't want you to be anxious. We would have all been there for you, and I'm sure there will be time to talk about that in the future. But today, I'd like just to enjoy having my friend back."

The waiter chooses that moment to set our drinks down. "Are you ready to order?"

"Sure," Charlotte jumps in. She picks up the menu and reads off her order. "I'll have the margarita pizza, and the super-greens healthy salad."

We spend the next hour chatting away about Charlotte's life over the last few years. Robert, her husband, sounds nice. They have a house in Bedminster and Charlotte was over-the-moon at the prospect of being a mother. I let her talk about everything and anything she wants. As long as the conversation isn't on the past, my feelings or what I've been doing all this time, I'm good.

The guilt and regret I had felt in the pit of my stomach before meeting her had slowly been replaced with a growing ache that had everything to do with not being able to have a family. It was wrong on so many levels, to resent that my friend—the one I'd only just got back—was happy and going to be a wonderful mother.

We go our separate ways after we polished off lunch. Jake is preoccupied the whole time we are in the restaurant and certainly seems happy that Charlotte has left, and we are free to go.

Despite his declaration this morning, there are going to be some big conversations in our future. Would he still love me knowing we'd never be able to have children of our own?

JAKE

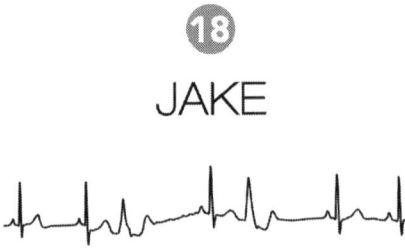

Of all the fucked-up coincidences, this had to happen today. *Shit!*

All the years I'd been a dick were coming back to bite me, spoiling the one thing I wanted. A future with Lily.

Yvonne recognised me the minute she saw me. It had only been a couple of years since I told her to get lost. Didn't stop her from trying to worm her way back in, though. She pulled some of her own stalker-shit before she finally got the message. Seeing her in the same room as Lily made me want to hit something very-fucking-hard.

I don't trust Yvonne as far as I can throw her. She is evil and twisted, and I'm pretty sure she doesn't have a good bone in her body. Her possessive streak is what finally made me cut off our hook ups. That and Andy's interest in her since his wedding. She'd sunk her claws into me when I was a kid and although I enjoyed the times we were together, I didn't want her anywhere near my life now. She represents everything I am that isn't good enough for Lily. But I've gotten past that. I fucking love her, and I'm going to be better for her.

I keep my eyes on Yvonne the entire time we are in the restaurant. She goes about her job, and I stay in my seat. I shoot down her only move toward me with a simple shake of my head. She responds best to a firm hand.

My phone vibrates in my pocket, and I'd put money on it

being Yvonne.

Don't want to introduce me to your friend?

Fucking bitch. I scroll through the contacts and find her name. I hit the delete contact option and shove my phone back into my pocket. I return to stalking her movements. She comes back onto the floor and does a piss-poor job of ignoring our table. She disappears again, and I feel my phone vibrate again.

I thought you only fucked women Jake? Moved on to actually dating have we? Seems that all the crap you gave me was you just using me, huh.

This time I block the number and hope Yvonne gets the message.

Lily and Charlotte are busy chatting away, and I'm happy to stay out of the conversation. I can keep an eye on my past while protecting my future.

I pay the bill the minute I can and usher Lily out and back to the car without incident. I can take a breath knowing we'll never come back here again, and I can keep Yvonne where she belongs, in my past.

It's not until we're in the car and travelling back that Lily breaks the silence.

"You were quiet at lunch."

"Sorry. It was time for you and Charlotte. I was happy to play the spare wheel."

"There wasn't something else on your mind? You didn't look very happy and you checked your phone several times."

"No, I'm good. Just want to get home." I wasn't about to tell her about Yvonne.

The journey back to London is quiet. Lily dozes, no doubt worn out by the emotionally challenging weekend. With a bit of luck, we can go home and just move on. I know there is still a long way to go, but I hope this was the hardest part. She's been so brave.

We stop at Reading for a coffee before tackling the London traffic.

"Are you going to drop me back at my flat?"

"No, I thought we could go back to mine. You've got some overnight stuff. And by the way, this is not just something I want for tonight. I want you with me every night."

"Jake, please. Can we not do this today? I'm exhausted and can't fight you."

"Well don't then."

"Hey, saying you love me doesn't give you permission to ride roughshod over me."

"I love you, and I want you with me. My place is bigger than yours. Keep yours, rent it out, whatever. But I'd like you to move in with me." She turns in on herself as if she's considering my request.

"I thought the deal was you'd leave the moving in idea if I came with you this weekend?"

"The deal changed when you said you loved me. So?"

"Maybe, but I'm not staying tonight. May I get some perspective and time to process this weekend?"

"I'll pick you up tomorrow after work. Around eight. You can pack your stuff."

LILY

I shut the front door and feel like collapsing for a week.

I dig in my bag to find my phone and fire an email off to my boss saying I've been sick and won't be in tomorrow. I head to the bedroom and fall onto the bed, exhausted from the emotional turmoil we've been through this weekend.

My entire world has shifted. The old Lily left yesterday morning, and a new Lily has returned. I'm a different person. I'm not sure who that person is, yet. Something Jake said struck me. He didn't want the old Lily. He didn't want the new Lily he met in a club. He wanted a happy Lily. Perhaps, now I've started to lay some old ghosts to rest, I could look at finding out who she was.

I roll over and stare at the ceiling. I wanted to smile. I felt… happy. I hadn't felt anything close to this in years, but there is still a part of my soul that tells me I shouldn't feel like this. Surely, I've been through enough? Surely, I can look to the future? Tim would want that. He wouldn't want me to drown in grief the rest of my life.

I get up from the bed and walk out to the kitchen. I pull open the fridge and grab a lonely can of Coke from the shelf. I set it down on the counter and look at the rest of my house. It is tiny really, nothing adds up to a home. No reason to stay. My mind replays Jake's order to move in with him, and a smile splits my lips. He makes me happy. Being with him makes me happy. It might be the craziest and stupidest thing in the world to jump right into living together, but I have to learn from my past—you don't know how long you have left.

I abandon the Coke on the side and go to retrieve my bag. I head to the Chinese take-away I'd often relied on to feed me. The girl behind the counter smiles in welcome, and I order a few of my favourites; sweet and sour chicken, mushroom chow mein, prawn toast and spring rolls.

Twenty minutes later I'm back in my house, my Chinese piled high in a dish, sitting in my favourite chair. This is going to be the last night in my little home. I may not have loved it, or put any identifying mark on it, but I'd sought refuge here. I had escaped, and it had hidden my secrets well. I'd been safe inside these walls.

I stuff myself with the delicious noodles and sit back feeling more positive and hopeful than I had since the accident. I know things wouldn't be easy, but I have people who love me. I'd underestimated what a positive influence they could have been when I ran. But I have a future that involves Jake and my parents and Charlotte. Hope is such a fragile thing.

Last night I was full of it. This morning, as the rain drowns out the sun, it is hard to feel so spritely. Am I crazy for thinking we can make this work?

Don't forget to pack baby. Jake

His text pulls a smile from me and I disregard my doubts. I want to live with him. I want to grab hold of the future that is within my reach, but I know I have one more secret to confess before I can take that step. If we are going to have any chance of surviving as a couple, I need to start with honesty. It might seem like some second-chance fairy tale, but it felt anything but.

I think we should talk before I move in, it's important.
Lily x

What's there to discuss. I love you. I'll pick you up later.

Jake

Jake, please. You need to know all the facts and I've not been completely honest with you. Just please, let's talk first. Lily x

I don't hear from him again for the rest of the day, and I try and keep my mind positive. I pull the suitcase out from under my bed and set about packing my few possessions and clothes. The choices of what to take have been reduced since my outburst a few weeks back. My 'whore uniform' remains in a black bag in the corner of the room. I won't be wearing those clothes again. I can't. That set of clothes can go out with the rubbish. The rest of the furniture can stay. I won't be selling this place. It might not serve as a good omen, but I won't risk my future on a relationship that might not last. Renting it out will certainly provide a tidy extra income. Jake's place must be a small fortune in comparison.

Two hours later, I'm ready to leave. It's sad to think five years can fit into a single suitcase. Maybe if Jake and I work, I could consider taking a few things out of storage.

I contact the agent I rented the property through and talk about putting the apartment back up for rent. I clean the bathroom and kitchen, but considering they are both too small to swing a cat in, it doesn't kill as much time as I'd hoped.

The clock moves at a perilously slow pace, drawing out every action and thought I have. My mind repeats the words I know I must say to Jake again and again. No matter which way I phrase it, it still boils down to the same fact. I can't have children. If he wants a family, then he needs to reconsider our future. Of course, there are other possibilities, but there will be time to consider that once we clear this hurdle.

The door opening snaps me out of my sad daydream, and Jake walks in.

My heart speeds up, and flutters in my chest as my stomach

drops away. None of the time spent pondering this is going to help now. I need to be honest and trust things will go my way.

"Are you packed, baby?" He looks around the front room that hasn't changed from when he was last here.

"Yes, but we do need to talk first." I unfurl my legs from the chair and stand up, taking his hand and leading him to the sofa.

"There isn't anything we need to discuss. God, haven't I said enough to you? Haven't I shown you how much I'll do for you?"

"This isn't all about you. This is something that can shape our future together and I have to be honest with you now, or we'll both live to regret it. Please?"

He sits back and drapes his arm over the back of the chair. His body language shouts he's not impressed, but at least he's going to listen. I look Jake in the eyes – his beautiful hazel eyes that reflect both warmth and aggression, strength and hurt.

"I told you about the accident. I told you about what happened in the crash and my recovery, but I left something out." I start my pre-rehearsed speech and try to focus on the words rather than their meaning. Giving voice to them, however, is harder than I thought. "My surgery was high risk. I was losing a lot of blood, and they had to go in and repair the damage. It didn't go according to plan. As well as the damage to my pelvis, my uterus ruptured, and I was haemorrhaging into my pelvic cavity." I drop my gaze. He's following the words, listening to what I'm saying but I know the final blow is coming. "They removed my uterus. That's one of the scars on my abdomen. I can't have children."

My shoulders sink as the strength I'd been clinging to evaporates with the words I've just spoken. He knows.

My vision blurs at the thought of losing Jake, but I know I've done the right thing. I look up and blink away the tears. His posture hasn't changed, but he now wears a contemplative expression that doesn't offer me immediate solace.

"You understand what I've said? What this means for us if we're going to have a future?"

"Yes."

"Do you… do you have anything to say?"

"You want me to decide, on the spot, now, if I want a family?" His voice is soft but shakes with tension.

"No, I just wanted you to know before I moved in. I couldn't start a life with you with this hanging over our heads. You deserve to know."

"Fuck!" He stands and runs his hands through his hair in frustration. "I love you. I'm pretty damn sure I've loved you my whole fucking life. I have no idea if a family is what I want. I have a pretty terrible one myself. I despise my brother, and my parents barely give me the time of day."

"I know, I'm sorry, but I couldn't…"

"Couldn't what? Have some fucking happiness in your life for once? Enjoy this moment we could share before dropping this on me?" Each word stabs me through the heart as if he physically took a sword to my chest. "I want you to be happy, Lily. I promised myself I'd work harder for you, that it was my time to do the heavy lifting like you did back in school to keep us together. But I have no clue what to do now. Are you saying you won't move in if I want a family with you?" His face contorts as if he's in pain.

"No, that's not it, I just needed for you to know that if children are what you want, in the future, then I won't be able to give them to you."

"And if I don't know?"

"Then we can discuss it when and if you're ever ready."

"What do you want?"

"Me?"

"Yes. You obviously have some feelings about this or you wouldn't have told me. Do you want kids? What if I don't? Is that going to be a problem for *you*?"

"I don't know," I mutter. Maybe I *was* hoping for a fairy tale and that everything would be alright. Jake wouldn't mind, and we'd deal with it in the future when we were stronger and when we knew each other better.

"Don't you think you should have an idea before you drop this on me and leave me to decide our future? So, tell me. Do you want kids?" he asks.

"Yes."

"Good. Are we done now? Or is there more?"

"Why are you being like this?"

He paces around the cramped room and aggression rolls off him in waves. He finally stops and gathers me into his arms.

"I'm sorry, Lily." He kisses the top of my head as he pulls me in closer to him. "You scared me shitless all day thinking about what you could possibly have to say to me that was such an awful secret I'd change my mind about us, and now you put me on the spot about kids—something that has barely crossed my mind. I think I have the right to be freaked out."

We stand in silence, clinging to each other, neither of us willing to break the quiet.

He finally pulls away, and I let him go. He heads towards my room and comes back in with my suitcase in hand.

"Ready?"

"Ready?" I frown.

"Yes, we're going. I love you." He says the words as if they were an explanation for everything. And maybe for him, they are.

JAKE

"I know it's only been a week, but we can't spend every minute with each other. Going out for a few drinks isn't going to hurt. I'll be here when you get back. Hopefully I'll be asleep, so please don't wake me." Lily smiles at me. "I trust you."

"You could come with me?" I know she's right. We'd gone from being two single people who did what they chose, to living with each other in record time.

"And sit around while you drink with your mates? How about we plan something in a couple of weeks?"

"Okay. If you're sure?"

"I am. Now go. I won't be the girlfriend who suddenly won't let you do anything without me."

"Fine. I won't be late." I kiss her softly—a reassuring kiss—or at least my idea of what reassurance would feel like.

Nick has been relentless in his pestering. Seems he missed trawling clubs with me. Too bad. That is all in my past now.

I agreed to meet Nick, but we weren't going to any of the clubs. A few beers in the local bar. That's what I told Lily and I sure as hell wouldn't be breaking my promises now I finally had her.

The bar's busy, but I don't see Nick when I arrive, so I order two pints and find a seat.

First round is on me. Jake

A few minutes later I see Nick walk in. "Hey, thanks Jake." He takes a seat and gulps a couple of mouthfuls of beer. "So, how you been? It's like you've upped and vanished these few weeks." Nick wipes at his nose with the back of his hand as his eyes roam around the bar.

"How much have you had?" I knew that Nick had a habit. I was the one who introduced him to the white stuff.

"Don't worry. Just a little to take the edge off. Besides, I'm meeting someone."

"Oh yeah? Who? If you had other plans, I'd have gladly stayed at home, mate."

"Look, I'm doing a favour for a friend. Well, Andy, actually."

"You're doing a favour for my fucking brother?"

"Relax man. He just wanted me to meet some girl and take her out. It's no problem. She won't be here for a while."

"Don't fucking mess around, Nick. You know Andy and I don't get along. You wanted me to come out for a drink tonight, so what the fuck is going on?"

"Hello, Jake."

I spin around and see Yvonne leaning against the pillar next to our table. She pulls out a chair and sits down, a shit-eating grin across her face.

"So, you guys know each other?" Nick looks between us.

I don't even try to hide how pissed-off I am. "What the fuck are you doing here?"

"I was in the neighbourhood and asked Andy if he knew anyone who could show me around a little, that's all." She turns to Nick. "Hi, Nick, I'm Yvonne. Thank you for agreeing to be my guide."

Nick ogled Yvonne like all his Christmases had come at once. "A pleasure to meet you."

"Stop!" I slam my palm down on the table. "I don't know what your game is Yvonne, but I told you before to leave me alone. If you're still fucking my brother, go and interfere with his life and leave me alone."

"I'm just…"

"You're just leaving. Don't fuck with me, Yvonne. Leave. I don't ever want to see you again. I thought I made myself pretty clear."

She stands up and runs her hands down her dress before stepping away from the table. "Very well, Jake. Have it your way."

She turns and leaves without pushing me any further.

"Was that necessary?"

"Yes. Believe me, you don't want to be messing around with Yvonne. If Andy has asked you to do him a favour by helping her out, he's still sleeping with her. There is nothing good about that woman."

"You can be a right cock block."

"Go find someone I don't hate to sleep with." I down the rest of my pint, in no mood to carry on this conversation. I should have stayed at home.

"Hey, look. I'm a little buzzed. Why don't I get you another pint and we call it quits? Then you can go home to Lily and I'll see if I can find myself a nice girl to cosy up to?"

"I'm not in the mood for anymore shit. One more pint then I'm gone."

"Great."

LILY

*I*t is early, but for some reason I'm shattered. The emotional ride I've been on the last couple of weeks has taken it out of me. I aimlessly flick through the channels on the television but nothing holds my interest. I hear a key in the lock and expect Jake to come through the door even though he's been gone for less than an hour. The fumbling continues but the door doesn't open so I get up to open it.

"Oh, thank you. My key must have gotten stuck." A blonde woman pulls a silver key from the door and waltzes past me.

"Excuse me, who the hell are you?"

"Well, I could ask you the same thing? I wasn't expecting Jake to have another woman here," the blond retorts.

"This is my home. I live here." I suddenly feel wide awake and very alive. Adrenaline surges through me as my mind reels with all the scenarios that could involve this woman and Jake.

"Really? You must be the flavour of the week." Her eyebrow arched. "Oh well... while the cat's away... I was hoping to surprise him."

"Who the fuck are you?"

"I'm Yvonne. Jake's girlfriend. Who are you?"

I feel the blood drain from my face as the words sink in. She must be lying, she must be. Jake loves me.

"There must be some mistake because *I* live here. Jake is *my boyfriend.*"

"Oh sweetie, is that what he told you?" She sways her hips as she takes a few steps closer towards me. She looks like an oversized Barbie with sticky lips that glisten too much. "We've been together for years—since he was in school in fact. I taught him everything he knows, especially how to fuck."

No, no, no, this can't be happening.

"Jake didn't date in school. He never had a girlfriend."

"I think I'd know, love. Clearly, he doesn't tell you everything. Now, I think this little game is over. I suggest you get your little butt out of here."

"Excuse me, no, just NO!" I was stronger than this. I'd been through hell and back, and I had the fucking scars to prove it. Whatever this was, it wasn't Jake. "This is my house. Jake is very much *my* boyfriend. If you think you can just sweep in here, say a few words to scare me off and cosy up to him, you can go to hell. You're the one who needs to leave. Now." My voice drips ice. My relationship with Jake may have its flaws; we may have a long way to go, but I know Jake loves me, and I know how much I love him.

I smile sweetly at the stunned look on Yvonne's face. If she thinks I'll accept her coming in with some bag of lies, then she has underestimated me.

"There's the door, Yvonne. I suggest you leave before I call the police and report an intruder."

"Oh really. Why don't you ask Jake about me? Ask him where he got his taste for rough sex. Or maybe ask him about his little coke habit. Do you know he likes to snort it off my tits before fucking me? He locks me in the bedroom for weeks at a time. He is that voracious and only I can satisfy him."

"Out… Out now." I wouldn't break, not in front of her. "Go now, or I phone the police." The cold look she gives me is nothing compared to the hurtful words she's thrown at me. Some of which I can't help but listen to. I snatch the key from her hand, and she leaves with a look that suggests I haven't seen the last of her.

I slam the door after her and hope there aren't any further visitors tonight.

I give myself a minute—because I think I deserve it—before heading back to retrieve my phone.

Who's Yvonne and why does she have a key to your place?
Lily

I'm on my way. Jake

Great. Fucking great.

JAKE

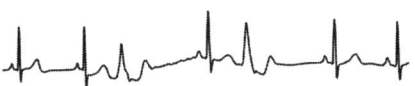

*A*ll my screwing around is about to rain shit down on my ass. God knows what lies Yvonne had been spouting to Lily. Or what truths for that matter. I didn't ever want Lily to meet Yvonne, and now she pulls this shit.

"Lily!" I shout as I barge into our apartment.

"I'm in the kitchen."

I walk in to see her standing by the stove, stirring a wooden spoon in a saucepan. "What are you doing?"

"I'm making myself a hot chocolate. I want something to calm me down."

I ease across the tiles towards her. I fight the urge to just hug her to me and promise nothing Yvonne said is true, but I know better than that. Lily deserves better.

"So… Yvonne. Where do you want to start?"

She looks up at me and I see the red rims around her eyes.

"Baby, I'm sorry. I don't know how she had my fucking key. I never gave her one."

"Well, I know you've got a history."

"I'm not going to lie. I used to sleep with her."

Lily pours the milk from the pan into a large mug and stirs several spoonfuls of powdered chocolate into it. She cups it in her hand and walks past me into the lounge. I follow, unsure of what I should say next.

Lily sits down and pulls her feet under her, still cradling the cup of warm chocolate. "How long?"

"How long what?"

"How long did you sleep with Yvonne?"

"Since school. It was never serious. She was a casual hook-up. She is friends with my brother, and she was convenient."

"Do you know how that makes you sound, Jake?" She turns to look up at me.

"Yes." I scrub my hands over my face. "You know very well I was never a saint." I perch on the chair opposite her.

"If you slept with her for years, she's probably in love with you."

"She saw us last week. In Bristol. She is a waitress at the restaurant where we met Charlotte. She messaged me but I ignored her. She showed up at the bar tonight. Nick said he was doing a favour for Andy by showing a friend around. I told her I never want to see her again."

"Your brother? What does he have to do with this?"

"He and Yvonne have history as well. I stopped seeing her a few years back when she started to get possessive and clingy. I found out that Andy was sleeping with her as well. No way I wanted to be a part of that."

"So, you shun her and ignore her in Bristol and she shows up here? What the hell, Jake?"

"I know it sounds bad."

"She sounds crazy."

"I had no idea she'd turn psycho and break in." I pause and wait for Lily to scream or shout. Nothing happens, she just sips her chocolate. It would be a lot fucking easier if she'd shout at me.

"How many more 'Yvonne's' am I going to confront? You know my secrets. You know the worst of me. I need to know the worst of you. I want to fight for us, so I need to know what I'm up against." She looks me in the eyes and I can see the hurt and doubt that Yvonne put there.

"Like what? And I never had a girlfriend. Not until you."

"Is there anything else I should know? Hidden pregnancies, debt, drugs? I want everything on the line."

"There are no hidden girls. Yvonne is the closest there ever was to someone in my life. I ended things with her years ago. She's playing some fucked-up game, that's all." I give Lily a pointed stare. "No pregnancies. The only debt I have is the mortgage on this place. I enjoyed coke on a night out. Yes, I got wasted and drunk and slept with countless girls, but no one was serious. You are my only addiction."

She turns away from me and finishes her chocolate.

"Do you want another drink?"

"No, I'm good thanks."

Fine. I retreat to the kitchen to get a handle on my feelings. I wrench the handle on the fridge and nearly pull it off its hinges. I grab a can of Coke from the door and slam it shut.

I head back to the sofa, sit down next to her and raise my arm in an invitation I hope she accepts. She snuggles across and tucks herself next to my body. I close my eyes in thanks at the small gesture.

"It's been a long fucking day."

"Yep."

"Are you still mad?"

"Yes."

"I'm sorry. What else do you want me to say."

"I'm not mad at you. I'm just mad at the situation. I was happy and…" She raises a hand and makes a futile gesture.

"You're so fucking strong, Lily. This is nothing."

She gives a little snigger.

"Just remember I love you. So fucking much. You're the only girl I've ever loved. That should be enough."

"Love is never enough, but it's a start."

LILY

"I promise, we won't have any more drama." Jake pulls me in tight against his chest and I try and relax into him.

"How do you know that?"

"Because I'd do anything to make sure you're happy, baby."

I let Jake's words sink in. They are everything that I once longed to hear from the boy I gave my heart to. I was finally happy. For a week. I'd thrown caution away and wanted to take charge of my happiness. My life is finally piecing back together. It feels like the glue is waiting to set, if anything knocks it, the pieces will break apart again, but I'll take it.

"Are you tired baby?"

"Not really."

"Do you want to go to bed?"

"To the same bed that you fucked Yvonne in? The same bed you kept her tied to for a week because you couldn't get…"

"Enough! I get the picture."

"I'm sorry. I just… when I think about you and her, my skin crawls." I get up and pace around the room. My limbs feel full of static as I try and reach the calm I want to achieve. Logically, I know I shouldn't hold Jake's past actions against him. But it's easier to think it than put it into action.

"What do you want to do?"

"I want to sleep."

"Come on then, let's go to bed." Jake stands up and rests his hands on my shoulders, halting my pacing.

"Fine."

Jake pulls me through into the bedroom and sets about undressing for bed. I slip under the covers and lie on my side facing away from Jake.

"Good night, baby."

"Good night."

His quiet voice comes out of the dark. "Tell me what you need and I'll do it."

"Don't hurt me. I don't want to be hurt anymore."

His arm tightens around my waist and pulls me to him in silent promise.

Sleep evades me, no matter how much I want to just drift away and forget about our unexpected visitor. I should have ignored the door. *Who the hell just opens a door without checking who could be standing behind it!* But as I think about how I could have avoided this evening, I wonder if I'd prefer to be ignorant about this part of Jake's past.

We both have a past, but we want to focus on a future. A future together. I was unable to fight for the life I had with Tim. I had to watch as he died inches away from me as I lay helpless and defenceless. This isn't the same. I can do something to protect myself and Jake. I can fight. I can stop being an insecure girl and acknowledge that our relationship isn't going to take a traditional path and if there are challenges in our way, we will overcome them.

As my mind focuses on all the things that are positive about being with Jake, a plan forms in my head that lets me chase the dreams I never dared to hope for. As I try and find some rest, the idea blossoms and takes root in my mind.

My family—my parents—were such a vital part of my life when I was younger. Tim expanded that family. Now I had a second chance at a family, and Jake was the centre of it.

My head feels groggy when I wake up. Not the bright morning start I was hoping for as I finally succumbed to sleep last night, or was it earlier this morning?

I turn over and reach out to Jake and find the warmth of his back. I stroke my fingers down his spine and inch my body closer to him. I didn't offer much in the way of reassurance as we went to bed last night and I regret that.

"Jake?"

"Mmm?"

"You awake?"

"I am now, baby." He turns over on his back.

"I'm sorry that I let us go to sleep unhappy. I had a lot of things to think about and I'm sorry if I acted coldly."

"You had every right to be upset after whatever that bitch said to you. Do you want a coffee?" Jake climbs out of bed and trudges to the kitchen before I've even answered.

I let him have his space. I needed mine last night and he didn't push. Now it was my time to let him be, even though I wanted to get to a place where I could ask him about my idea.

He comes back in and deposits a mug of coffee on the bedside table. "I'm going to head to the gym for a bit."

"Okay."

"You can come and swim if you want, but I need to just... do something." He grabs his gym bag from the corner and stuffs a clean set of workout clothes into it. He changes and comes back to kiss my forehead before leaving the room. No more words, no explanation. The bang of the door slamming shut echoes around the apartment—the apartment I no longer want to stay in.

I fall back into the covers and stare at the ceiling. I'd have to be patient with Jake, or at least try to be.

A few hours later Jake blows back in and marks his return with a loud slam of the door.

"Hi!" I call.

"Hi." He finds me in the lounge and crashes down next to me on the sofa.

"Are you feeling better?"

"I wasn't feeling bad."

"You sort of ran off to the gym as soon as you were awake."

"I go to the gym a lot."

"I know. I was just asking if you were feeling better?"

"And I said, it was nothing."

"Fine. Good. I want to talk to you about something—an idea I had last night."

"If it's to do with Yvonne, then can we just forget about her for today. Every time I think about her I get the urge to hit something."

"It's not about Yvonne directly, but she is part of what's on my mind."

"Come on Lil, enough with the riddles."

"Fine." I swivel so I'm looking at him. "I don't want us to stay here anymore. We both have demons haunting us. I think we need a clean break."

"A break? From us? Lily, you're not making sense."

"Not from us. I want us to have our own place. Together. I don't want to be thinking about any other girl who might come bursting through with a key, or the countless girls you've fucked in the bed we now share. I want to make a fresh start where we make our own memories without anything tainted." As soon as I say the words, I know it's the right thing for us to do. "I want us to buy a house together."

"What, just find a new place to live?"

"Yes. Why not?"

"You're crazy."

"No. I want us to have the best shot of an actual us. So far we've fucked about, hurt each other, been confronted with ghosts, and we're barely holding it together."

"Look, I know things haven't been straightforward…"

"Huh, we're about as far from straightforward as you can get. But I want that to change."

He circles me so we're facing one another.

"Can you just hold on a minute. Last week you were telling me we couldn't have kids and made me decide on the spot if that was something I wanted with you. Now, you're ready to buy a house together?"

"I think it's the right thing to do. And I'm not sure how I feel about staying here while we house hunt. At the very least, we're getting a new bed."

"You're serious. You want us to move?" His eyes spit anger in my direction, and I shudder, thinking I may have pushed him too far.

"I think we should take this as an opportunity. You've got me this far. You wanted to live together, what's the problem with owning a house as well?" He doesn't answer and just looks at me like I've grown a second head. "Are you going to say anything?"

"Just like that? Lily, come on," he calls after me as I wander into our bedroom.

"What's wrong with the idea of having a house *together*?" I shout back at him.

I hide under the pillow. A feeling of exhaustion ebbs through me that has nothing to do with the lack of sleep I've suffered over the last few days.

I hear the door to the apartment slam. He's left again.

Perhaps the timing was a little out of left field, but this was the right thing to do. This is what we needed.

* * *

"Lily, I know you're not asleep."

"Oh?"

"Yeah. It's two in the afternoon."

"That doesn't mean I couldn't be asleep."

"Well, you're talking now so clearly you're not asleep."

I fling the pillow from my head and peek at Jake. Sweat coats his skin and dampens his temples.

"Did you go back to the gym?"

"No, running. I needed to work off some steam.."

My heart squeezes in my chest. "I thought that was what this morning was for?"

"It didn't work."

"Go grab a shower and then come back." I smile. Sure enough, Jake heads to the bathroom and takes no time cleaning up. I lift the duvet in invitation when he walks back into the bedroom. He's changed into a plain t-shirt and shorts but doesn't take them off before climbing under the covers.

His heart hammers against my ear as I rest my head on his chest.

"It's been a pretty crappy few days."

"Yes," I agree. "I'm sorry I sprung the moving thing on you. Honestly, I hadn't considered it before but the idea came to me last night and it just overtook me. When I woke up this morning, I still wanted it. I still want a fresh start with you. Very much."

"I'm sorry I've put you in the middle of my crap. I warned you, Lily. I told you I'd never be good enough for you."

"Shut up, Jake. You don't get to pull that with me now. Not after everything we've been through." I can't let him think like that and realise that I need to put his past behind me as well.

I run my hands over his muscled chest and turn his chin so he's looking at me.

"I love you."

"I love you, too."

He rolls his body so he's positioned over me, pressing me into the mattress before his lips slam into mine. He pins me with his ferocity before he relaxes and lets our lips slide together. I wrap my legs around his and try and connect us as closely as possible. Right now, we both need to take comfort in one another, and I put as much feeling into each touch as I can.

His warm body cocoons me in his strength. I trace the muscular plains of his back. My fingers work their way to the edge of his t-shirt and tug it until he gets the hint. He breaks our kiss and kneels, giving me a delicious view as he reveals each sculpted muscle. I scamper to rid myself of my sweater and bra as Jake watches.

Right now, I want to forget that anything else exists other than me and Jake. I lean up and my lips set to work across his stomach, kissing and licking as I go. Jake groans in appreciation, and it spurs me on. My hands slide up his toned thighs and rest on the elastic waist of his shorts. I inch them down, revealing another portion of skin for me to worship.

"Lily, I want to fuck your mouth, baby. So fucking bad."

I free his stiff cock and begin to tease the fat head with feather-light kisses. I flick my tongue against his slit and lave the underside until he breaks. Jakes hands grip my head, and he thrusts his hips telling me just what he wants. I oblige and let him push to the back of my throat on a strangled groan.

"Jesus!"

He sets the pace, surging into my mouth before I can relax. I keep my tongue sliding around his cock as he slips in and out. I focus on pulling air in through my nose and not gagging as he presses as far as he can. My hands cling to his legs to keep stable. As much as I want him to forget about everything apart from me, I want him to fuck me and not just my mouth. I fight against his hold and suck his cock like a lollypop until I can pull him free of my mouth.

"Not in my mouth," I pant. "I want you in me."

He pushes me back down before divesting me of my knickers. He removes his shorts and seeks my lips again. Our tongues and teeth collide in a fit of lust and passion as we both seek to rid ourselves of the events of the last few days.

His hand cups my sex before he slides a finger deep inside me. I'm already wet for him, and it doesn't stop Jake from driving me to distraction. I close my eyes and enjoy every touch. His ministrations spark the first rumblings of my pleasure as he sweeps over the sensitive nub of my clit. Heat wraps me in desire as I yearn for more attention. His thumb presses down as he pushes his finger deeper to massage my G-spot. My legs quiver in anticipation.

"Don't make me come," I beg.

"I'll make you come, baby. Just not with my hand."

"Please, take me!"

Jake spreads my legs making room for him. He guides his cock to my entrance before rising and thrusting as deep as he can. I gasp at the intrusion but adjust quickly as he stills and drops his head to the crook of my neck.

"You feel so good, baby. I love you."

"I love you. Now, move. I want you to fuck me."

"Jesus, you're perfect." His hot breath tickles my neck, and a smile spreads across my lips.

Jake takes his time, slowly dragging back and forth and hitting every nerve and sensitive inch of flesh until I want to scream in pleasure. I focus on his hazel eyes and try to calm my thrumming heartbeat. His rhythm keeps me on the edge of bliss, and I score his back in frustration. My fingers dig in, and I pull him closer to me as I push my hips up to meet his.

We abandon the steady pace and become a tangle of sweat

covered limbs as we fight for release. I can feel the energy between us as the air grows heavy with the sounds of our desire. Our groans and gasps offer an erotic soundtrack to our love making. This is what we need—a connection that ties us together so we can overcome the world.

With every thrust and grind, my release builds in the pit of my stomach. It shorts out any rational thought I have left.

"Tell me you're about to come because I'm so fucking close!" Jake grunts.

"Yes… Just a bit… more." I wrap my legs around his waist and pull him in closer. It triggers the rush of my climax as my body arches into Jakes and pulses in rapture. My body goes limp as I let my limbs recover. Jake drives into me and stills as he comes, collapsing into the pillow next to my head.

The mingled in and out of our breaths fill the air as we both recover. Goosebumps cover my chest as the sweat cools on my exposed skin. For however long it lasts, we are just us. We don't need to worry or concern ourselves with the rest of our lives. We are two people in love. Nothing else matters.

"I love you, Lily," he pants.

"I love you, Jake."

21
LILY

My alarm blasts from the bedside table, and I curse as sleep deserts me.

"Come on sleepyhead."

"Shut up. It's too early."

"It's not. I'm heading straight to the office. It's about an hour past when you'd normally be at the pool swimming."

I spring into action at Jake's announcement. If I'm not careful, I'll be late. Not that it will matter soon.

"I'll see you tonight," I call to Jake as I rush to the bathroom. "We can talk this evening."

"About what?" He puts his head around the door and watches as I strip and jump in the shower.

"The future."

"You were serious yesterday?"

"Yes."

"I thought it was just a reaction to everything that happened over the weekend?"

"No."

"No?"

"That's right. My mind hasn't changed. I still want us to look for a new place." I watch as emotions flick across his face and distort the peace that was there. His brows scrunch into a scowl as he observes me through the glass.

"We need to talk about this. You can't just make a decision

like this."

"Okay," I concede. Now is not the time to get into another argument.

He leaves, and I get on with my routine, minus the swim. I grab my gym kit as I don't want to forego all exercise and leave.

I hurry into the office and slide behind the reception desk. I fire up the computer and print off the itinerary for the day. Nothing is keeping me at this job. This is not what I spent years at university for. It isn't what I want to do with my life, but when I'd left home, I'd left everything—including my career.

There were days, and even weeks, when I'd get by on doing the bare minimum. I hadn't felt the drive to succeed or do well professionally since I left Bristol. What was the point? I had nothing to work towards so I played it safe. Walking in here today is the first time in years that I feel energised to do something. That something is to resign, so I am free to move on.

I smile as I print my resignation letter. I seal it in an envelope addressed to my boss and leave it on the edge of my desk to deliver later today. I check the diary and make sure the conference room is ready before opening up my old email account. I search through my contacts for my old physio boss. I worked under Holly while I was at the Bristol Royal Infirmary. She was a great mentor and physio. If my plan is to work, I'll need some assistance from her.

When I decided to leave Bristol, I sent in my resignation and left my career behind with everything else. Since then, I've let my registration with the HCPC lapse so I can't go back to being a physio even if I want to. Not straight away, anyway.

It will be a long shot, finding a job after such a gap on my CV, but with my thoughts now focused on a positive future I want to try.

Over the course of the day I go about finding the relevant information I need to make my re-admission to the HCPC register.

I'll need to complete some supervised practice and update my skills but that should be fine.

By the end of the day I have a plan in place. I leave work feeling lighter, like I've shed an invisible weight I've been carrying around all these years. The feeling is incredible considering the weekend and the past few weeks we'd had. A younger Lily, a Lily who hadn't survived heartbreak, would be looking at all of the reasons why the plans I am making are all too spontaneous, too rash.

I can't afford to think like that anymore. Who knows what life will deal me next? I'd played it safe in the past and always done the right thing in life. Now it is time to take a risk and gamble on love and get my life back on track.

The bustle of the evening rush hour pulls me along on my journey home. I enter the gym and ensure that I get in a good run to make up for my absence this morning. Jake has a treadmill at home but that's his thing, and I've been sleeping much better while in his bed. Perhaps my daily punishment through cardio could let up?

I skip the shower and head for home in my running gear. I round the corner, eager to talk to Jake about his day.

The move to Jake's increased my walk home from the gym. By the time I turn onto our road, I'm exhausted. I dig around in my bag for my keys and look up to see Yvonne walking out of the front door of our building and pacing the pavement.

My pulse sprints to life as I freeze in place. *Why would she be in our building? Was she seeing Jake?* I suck in a deep breath and march towards her. She sees me approach and despite our previous confrontation, greets me with the same false smile.

"You still around? I thought you would have realised you'll never have him." She has the nerve to look smug like she's got the upper hand here.

"No, I think you're sorely mistaken. You're the delusional one, and I suggest you leave."

Her smile flickers, clearly not getting the rise out of me that she had hoped for. "Aren't you worried what he'll do behind your back? What he's *already* done?" She licks her glossed lips and arches her brow.

"No." I insert as much confidence and assurance as I can, and it is precisely what I need to do. Yvonne's façade crumbles . She'll never win this battle. Not with me.

"You'll never be able to trust him. He'll treat you like dirt and never love you."

"Then why are you here, trying to run me off?" I challenge.

"You can't give him what he…"

"Stop! Just forget it, Yvonne. He loves me. I'm not about to condemn him because he has a past. I have a past, too, and frankly, it's none of your damn business. You can try and make me the insecure girlfriend, but I'm not that girl. So I suggest you run along." I make a shooing motion with my hand. "Go on. Shoo."

Her mouth opens and closes like a fish gasping for air.

"I never want to see you again." I grit out the words. She trembles with anger, but I stare her down, and she drops her gaze. She glances past my shoulder and turns on her heel before vanishing amongst the passers-by.

"Lily?" Jakes voice rings out. I turn and see him striding towards me, sublime in his crisp suit. Just seeing him helps to calm me after the adrenaline riddled showdown.

"Was that Yvonne?" His eyes turn murderous as he scans the road where she escaped. "What the fuck did she want?"

"Why don't we get upstairs?" Weariness saturates my voice. I have to pull him inside, as he's still searching the sea of people walking past. "Forget about her. Come on." I yank his arm and snap him out of his focus.

I can see the strain lingering around his eyes even after I've shut the door to the outside world. I want to comfort him and reassure him. He is the strength I didn't know I needed, and it's my time to show him what his love means to me.

JAKE

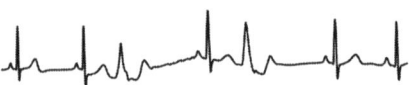

*J*am furious. She hasn't taken the hint and now she's back, trying to mess with Lily again. There are quite a number of people in my life that I don't like. I reserve the word hate for only a few, but right now, her name tops that list.

"Jake, you listening?"

"Sorry, what?"

Lily smiles at me. Thank God she's here because I don't want to think about what I would have done to Yvonne if she wasn't.

"I asked if you want a drink? Come on. You need to relax."

"I'm fine."

She huffs at me and makes an adorable attempt at telling me she's not buying my brush off.

"What?" I need to go for a run. I stalk off to the bedroom and rip my tie from around my neck.

"I understand if you feel angry. But there is nothing that she can say that will make me doubt us. I love you, and I'm not going to have her tear us down after we've only just found each other again."

I hear her words and try and let them calm my mind. I continue to strip out of my suit and grab a t-shirt and shorts from my bottom drawer.

"Are you even listening to me?"

"Yes." I was, I just didn't know what she wanted me to say.

"Jake!"

"What?" I stand, shirtless and facing her in the bedroom.

"What do you want me to say? That I can't stand the thought of Yvonne anywhere near you? That I hate that I used to try and forget about you by fucking her?"

"I know all of that, Jake. It doesn't change how I feel about you."

"Well, it fucking should. You're too good for all of this crap in your life. Everything about my life is dark, or dirty or turns to waste. I don't want that for you. You deserve better."

"You don't get to decide that, and you shouldn't have made that choice for me all those years ago either. You knew how I felt about you. Don't you think I had the right to decide how and who I spent my life with?"

"I would have ruined you, Lily. I still could."

"I'm not going to let anything ruin us. I keep trying to get it through your thick skull that I'm not that same girl."

"Well, it's pretty hard to break the habit of thinking of you like that." I lower my volume and breathe heavily. I was fired up before our little run in, and now adrenaline swamped my system. I turn and march past Lily on the way out of the bedroom and jump on the treadmill.

I stab the buttons on the console and set the machine in motion, jogging at a steady pace before I ease it up to a punishing speed. I need to tame this aggression and wrath that is constantly present. It has been on overdrive for the last couple of days. My muscles relax into the rhythm as I focus on running. I don't want to think, I don't want to feel, I just want to be happy with Lily.

Sweat trickles from my brow as I force my body to run harder and I find myself wondering if I will ever be rid of the underlying temper I've always had to keep in check. My legs protest at the pace I'm putting them under so I slow down, heaving oxygen into my lungs. I rest my head trying to find a sense of relief and calm until I turn around and see Lily waiting for me with a towel in her hand.

"Feel better?"

Did I feel better? No. I wanted to fuck her until I forget about the past. "No, but I'm sure I can think of something that will help." Sex was the one thing that calmed my nerves, and with Lily, it was fucking fantastic.

"No. I'm not going to sleep with you when you're like this. Not now."

Her simple refusal stuns me.

"No?"

"No. You're angry and upset, and I'm not going to help you push it all aside by letting you do to me what you've done to countless other women. Not now."

"So, no sex."

"No. Not even an hour ago you said that I was too good for you, and I deserved better. Well, how about you show me that person."

My teeth clamp together in frustration. I have no clue what she's trying to accomplish, but it certainly hasn't helped how I'm feeling. I grab the towel from her and head for the shower. A cold one, because my cock seems to have a one-track plan when Lily was around.

She is right. Treating Lily like all the girls before her is exactly why I'd avoided having any relationship with her. I'd already fallen into using her to sooth my agitated and maddened mood. I need to get my shit together.

The cold blast of water helps put a halt to any idea my cock had about Lily, and I let the ice water chill me to the bone. I want a break from my demons. I'd hidden them for years. I'd coped for years, and now I was ready to bury them. Preferably with a shovel, but I'd settle for a less violent option. It was the only way I could think to make things work with Lily.

Starting again, having a clean break was the right thing for us. For starters, we wouldn't have Yvonne dropping in at the odd hour.

I remain under the spray for as long as I can stand before my teeth start chattering. I grab a towel and dry off, rubbing some heat back into my limbs.

Lily is sitting on the sofa when I finally emerge.

"Have you thought about where?" I ask.

"Where what?"

"Where we'd move to?"

"Maybe Epsom or Kingston upon Thames. I know you'll need to commute, but I'd really like to get out of the city. I want this to be a move for our future together. Plus, it needs to be close to a hospital."

"Hospital?" She's not making sense.

"I've made enquiries about getting re-registered as a physio."

"That's great news."

"We need to sell both properties. If we're doing this, then it's all in. I don't want you keeping your place as a safety net."

"Fine. I don't want something to fall back on either." Her face lights up with the news, and it banishes the last of the cold still clinging to me.

"Are you serious?"

"About us? Totally."

She leaps from her seat and flings her arms around my neck, pressing her body against mine. Her smile, her giggly laugh, and her sheer happiness, warm a place in my chest and offer me peace.

22

LILY

Three weeks later

Normal, everyday errands fill the weeks. There are no surprises from ex-girlfriends. Maybe we'd made it through the storm. I keep my fingers crossed.

I went back home to see my parents on the weekend. I convinced Jake that he could let me do it on my own this time. He's been sulking since, which just reminds me of what he was like when we were at school.

Since he made the announcement that we could move, I wanted to let Mum and Dad know but felt I owed them a delivery of that news in person. There is still a long way to go with mending the hurt I'd caused over the last few years, but I want to work at it. Maybe someday we'll be living closer to home.

The last obstacle to the resolution of all our remaining issues is Jake's family.

If I could click my fingers and mend the rift between them, I would. Of course, I'd never met them so had no idea if they were the monsters I'd only glimpsed as a child. He, like me, moved for a reason. He forced me to face up to my past. I wasn't as confident in making him face his, but I want to try and help him to build bridges.

My apartment is on the market. Jake's had sold two days after putting it up for sale, so we had to move pretty quick. Next week

I'd be finishing work, and by pooling the money from the sale of both properties, we hoped to be mortgage free.

That doesn't brighten Jake's outlook on the whole plan though. He isn't going to settle for a house that he doesn't love. According to him, we'll be living in my apartment until he finds something he's happy with.

"Have you looked over any of the houses I've marked up?"

Jake is flicking the screen of his iPad at the breakfast bar. "There's only one I like," his answer doesn't hold any sign of real interest.

"Okay, so shall we try and get a viewing? I know the market's moving really fast."

"Sure. Set it up."

Jake's less than enthusiastic about anything to do with the move and I have to resist the urge to push him. "Are you going to tell your family that we're moving?"

"When I'm ready."

"Do you want to tell me when that might be? What about your brother?"

"I'm pretty sure he's the reason that Yvonne has been skulking. I'm fed up with his shit. I've taken it for years. He's not getting away with involving Nick this time. No fucking way."

His words worry me. My visions of any form of reconciliation clearly aren't shared.

"What are you going to do?" my voice shakes with nerves. It seems to snap him out of his internal focus.

"Come here." He gestures to me by holding his arms out. "It won't be anything less than he deserves. A few home truths. I want to make it clear to both him and my parents what kind of person Andy is. If Lisa is there, all the better."

"Are you sure you want to do that?" No matter what Andy's done, did he deserve to be called out in front of his family?

"You don't get a vote on this, Lily."

"Okay. It's your family."

"How about you? Have you heard back from your last boss about work experience or whatever?"

"Yes, she said that she'd be more than happy to offer me some supervised practice study. It would be unpaid and in Bristol, but it will help with my reapplication."

"What about jobs? Anything?"

"No physio openings, no. Holly said that she'll keep an eye out as well, but it might be a while until I'm back working again."

"There's no rush. I'm just pleased your talking about this again. You'd worked so hard to start your career."

"I know. And it's the first time in years that I'm looking forward to something again."

"I'd be more than happy for you to dedicate yourself to me." Jake grabs me around the waist and seeks out my lips.

"I would have thought moving in and buying a house together would be enough of a dedication." I giggle as Jake continues to rain kisses over my face.

"Well, you know my priorities. If I make you happy, I'll settle for that." He kisses the top of my head and tucks me against his chest.

JAKE

Six weeks later

When you have to work for something, it makes it that much better when you finally succeed. There are a handful of times when this applied to me: my degree, my first job placement, my move to head up the corporate law at Ross and Wheats, buying my first house and now buying this house with Lily.

My life has completely changed over the last couple of months, and it is all because of Lily. She's worked her gorgeous arse off to make our new start happen. She is determined to get us into our new house as fast as humanly possible. Of course, the closer we get to accomplishing our goal, the closer I get to facing my brother.

"You alright, baby?" Lily wraps her arms around my waist as we stand in the kitchen of our empty house, looking out into the garden.

"I'm good. Just thinking about the last few months. Thank you for making this happen."

Lily had fallen in love with this house in Surbiton, which pretty much sealed the deal. I have to admit I like it as well. It will take a bit of getting used to. The amount of space we have is massive compared to the small apartments in Shoreditch. We've settled for three bedrooms and no mortgage, something Lily seemed insistent on. The smallest bedroom will be my make-shift gym and the second bedroom will be a spare room for guests—at least for the time being.

The biggest perk of the new move is that Lily is with me, happy, and standing by my side.

"I can finally take my things out of storage," she muses.

"You can."

"I can't believe we've done all of this. We have a house. Together."

"Pretty incredible, isn't it?"

Lily twists in my arms and slams her lips against mine, knocking the air from my lungs. She's vicious and punishing and sends all my blood straight to my cock.

Her hand reaches between us, and she moves to unbuckle my belt.

"Wow, baby."

"Shh. This is our house, and I want to christen it. Now."

Oh God, I love this woman.

She frees my cock, and her delicate hand grips my length firmly, sliding up and down. Every muscle in my body comes alive at her touch. I break from our kiss and scan the room. Fucking her against the wall was my only thought as I pick her up and carry her the few meters before slamming her back against it.

Her legs wrap around my waist as her hungry eyes eat me up. There was a reason I loved dresses. I slide my arm along her bare thigh and hold her arse, gripping her tightly. She pulls me closer as her lips and teeth go to work on my neck.

She drives me fucking crazy when she's like this. Pumped up and fucking horny.

"Baby, you got to calm down, or this is going to be over way too fast."

"We've got all the time in the world," she purrs.

It kicks me into action, and I shove her underwear to the side as I lean my body against her, pinning her to the wall.

"Hold on, Lily," I growl. I unzip, shove my trousers down

and rub the head of my cock through her pussy. As I press into her entrance, her heat fires through my body. I pull her down as I thrust up to meet her. She tilts her head back and sighs in pleasure. It's the most satisfying sound, hearing her cries and moans as I fuck her and make love to her.

I capture her lips with mine, and we find a rhythm, both of us moving to elicit the most pleasure possible. My thighs burn as I drive into her, shoving her up the wall with each thrust. Lily breaks our kiss and her eyes close, shielding me from seeing her at her most vulnerable. I don't need her eyes to tell me how much she feels me anymore. I know she loves me.

"Is this what you wanted, baby? Me to fuck you in our new home?"

"Yes!" Her cry echoes loudly in the empty room.

"I'm going to do this to you in every fucking room. And that massive bed you ordered? You're not getting out of it unless I say. Understand?" I grunt my words as climax tingles my spine.

"Yes, oh, god, yes!" Lily stutters as she comes around my cock, sending her body into spasm. She flinches and moans in my arms as I chase my climax.

I follow after her. My orgasm shakes my body and turns my limbs to mush. We breathe together, out of breath from the erotic exertion. Her legs slide from my waist and we both crumple onto the floor.

I wrap her in my arms and stare up at the ceiling.

I've done it. I've got the girl I love, in a house we own and we're ready for a future together. Right now I feel on top of the fucking world. At least I will be after I recovered from the hot sex. *God, my life is good.*

LILY

Hostility rolls in waves from Jake as we take the short drive to his parent's house. I hadn't mentioned it again since he told me he'd do this when he was ready. I'd never met his parents and didn't know what to expect.

"They will seem nice. Mum will probably be all over you."

"Okay."

He tightens his stranglehold on the wheel as we turn onto a quiet street not far from my parents. He parks on a gravel drive that leads to a house that dwarfs anything I'd imagined.

"You lived in a mansion?" I squeak out.

"Appearances can be deceiving." Jake exits the car and comes around to open my door. He takes my hand and holds it in a death-grip as we head up to the front door. He knocks and then enters, calling his welcome as he does.

I expect his mum to greet us, but the hall is quiet as Jake pulls me through the house. We enter the lounge where his mum and dad are sitting cosily on one of the three sofas arranged in the middle of the room. His brother, Andy, and his very pregnant wife are in one of the other sofas.

"Oh, hi darling. Good to see you." His mum acknowledges Jake with a brief turn of her head. His dad barely looks up from his iPad as he's busy tapping away on the screen.

"Mum, Dad, this is Lily, my girlfriend. We have some news."

"Hi," I venture, feeling completely out of place. Neither his mum or dad really acknowledge me and my nerves start to take hold. Jake moves to seat us on the sofa, but his mum halts us in our tracks.

"Oh, well before that, as you're up, be a dear and put the kettle on, would you? Hello, Lily."

"Hello." I spy the tray on the centre coffee table filled with empty teacups and saucers.

"I don't think we'll be here that long." Jake replies.

"Really, Jake. Where are your manners? You come all the way here from Shoreditch and you won't even stay long enough to have a cup of tea?" She sniffs. "Andy's been telling us how rude you were to one of his friends."

My eyes widen in astonishment at her version of events. She must be referring to Yvonne.

Jake's fingers crush mine, trapped in his hand. I sit on the edge of my chair desperate to set her straight.

"Lily," he growls in warning.

"Andy's told us about you, Lily." His mum stands and comes to hug me to her. I stiffen and keep my hand locked in Jake's for support. "So, tea?" she asks me while turning towards Jake. Her hint isn't subtle.

Jake sits beside me on the remaining free couch and ignores his mother. Right now, I don't want him to leave me alone with his family.

It's the most bizarre atmosphere. Andy just smirks at me. Lisa, his wife, looks content and utterly oblivious, and his dad has barely raised his eyes from his screen.

"Really, Jake. I ask you to do one thing..." His mother taps her husband's knee. "Douglas, will you go and put the kettle on as Jake seems to think he's above that simple job."

His dad gives Jake a hateful look before silently leaving the room. I don't think I've ever felt more uncomfortable, but there was something his mother said that I can't ignore.

"Excuse me, Mrs. Stewart, but what did you mean by Jake being rude to one of Andy's friends? Clearly, Andy doesn't really know what she is like."

"I don't know what you think you know..." She bristles visibly.

"There is no *think* about it. I've met the woman." Her face reddens at my challenge. Jake squeezes my hand and pulls me back towards him.

"I think that's between me and Jake and has nothing to do with you." Andy pipes up and smirks at Jake.

"Andy, I don't know what crap you've been spouting, but I'm pretty fucking fed up with everything."

"Jake!" His mother's shock is almost comical. "You have no right to talk to Andy like that."

"I have every fucking right. I won't have Andy wilfully sabotaging my relationship with Lily." Astonishment crosses all of their faces. His dad has just entered with a pot of tea.

"Douglas, are you going to let him talk to me or Andy like that?"

"Don't worry, we're not staying. I thought I'd give this one more try. For Lily really, but I shouldn't have bothered. It's up to Andy to fill you in on what his 'friend' is really after. Unlike him, I have some respect for the word brother, even if he shows none to me."

Jake stares at Andy and tension vibrates in the air around us. I wait for either of them to say anything further, but they don't. I'm ready for an explosion from Jake, but it doesn't come. No hateful words shouted in spite. The way he's been treated makes me furious. How Jake has remained calm is beyond me.

He takes my hand and leads me out of one of the most ludicrous situations I've been in. I don't dare open my mouth. I'm not sure what I'd say if I did. I can see why Jake doesn't have the same relationship I have with my parents.

"Jake, wait," Andy calls as we crunch across the gravel drive.

Jake turns to stand off against his brother.

"Thank you. For not outing me in front of Lisa." Andy looks relieved.

"I didn't do it for you. And believe me, I'd love to finally knock that smug look off your fucking face. Are you still seeing Yvonne?"

"That's none of your business."

"Then you deserve everything you get. You might want to think about your wife and child in all of this. You helped Yvonne try and fuck up my world. I doubt she'd think twice about doing it to you."

"I can handle her. After all, this all started with me. You were just a happy diversion. Have to say, she's a fucking riot in bed. I won't be giving that up anytime soon."

"If that's the way you feel, then maybe you're perfectly suited. Come on, we're leaving." Jake opens the car door, and I scoot inside. "No... No... I can't." Jake turns around and heads back to Andy. "I just have one thing I require."

"And what's that?"

"Stay out of my fucking life."

I gasp at the right hook Jake slams into Andy's face. The thud is audible from inside the car. Andy spins backwards and stumbles to the ground clutching his face.

"If you ever try and interfere with my life again, then I won't be so generous. I'll make sure that your wife finds out exactly who Yvonne is." Jake turns to me and winks before climbing into the car and revving the engine.

I can't help but smile at the way Jake took him down. He deserved it and much more.

I don't need Jake to tell me we wouldn't be seeing his family again, and I had a sudden and powerful urge to go and visit my parents and tell them how much I loved them. The tragedy in my past had made me very aware of how short life could be and that every opportunity had to be taken. I didn't want to waste the second chance I had at a happy future. I reach my hand to cover Jake's over the gear stick.

"Can we stop at my parents? After that experience, I need to give them both a hug."

"Sure."

My heart breaks for Jake, but I'll make certain he doesn't feel like he is missing anything from his life. My parents already think he is marvellous. He'd brought me back to them, so he'd earned all the respect he'd ever need from them.

"Are you alright?" I have to ask.

"I might need some ice for my hand. Fucking kills."

I snort a giggle and relief floods me. "I'm sure we can manage a pack of peas. Jake?"

"Yes, baby."

"I love you."

"I love you, too."

"I promise I'll be all the family you'll ever need."

"I know. And I hope I can be everything you ever need."

"You already are."

EPILOGUE

LILY

One year later

"Please come and sit down. The cushions look fine. The house is fucking spotless."

"I want to make a good impression."

"I know, baby. And we will. They said this was more of a formality."

"What's the time?"

"Lily, please just calm…" The doorbell interrupts Jake, and I rush out into the hall to answer it.

A short, plump lady greets me with a stern look on her face. "Miss Hill?"

"Yes. Please, come in." I open the door wider to allow her entry. She takes a tentative step inside and looks around the hall. I lead her into the lounge where Jake is waiting.

"Hi, I'm Jake Stewart." Jake offers the lady his hand, and she beams back at him. Clearly, she agrees with my man choice.

We all take a seat, and I perch on the edge of the sofa, too anxious to fully relax. This woman could turn down our application. I'd fallen in love with Bella the moment I met her. Her big soft brown eyes pleaded with me to take her home. My heart melted then and there. She would be ours. As long as everything today went well.

"This is your first home visit?" The woman pulls out an official looking clipboard from her bag and sets about scanning the paperwork attached to it.

"Yes. We were told this was just a final check."

Shrewd eyes peer at me over the edge of the paperwork, and I have to fight against my reaction to shrink back into the sofa.

"Shall we get started? I need to have a tour of the downstairs and the garden, please."

I jump out of my seat, eager to please the woman who stands between me and Bella.

"The dining room is through there." I point out the other reception room before moving onto the kitchen.

"This is the kitchen. As you can see, we have plenty of space and the glass doors lead out onto the back garden which is completely fenced for security." I walk around the solid oak table to open the patio doors that allow us to spill out onto the deck and into the garden.

"Have you left an item of clothing with Bella so she will become familiar with your smell?"

"Yes, yes, we did that last time we visited."

"And have you considered how you'll look after her for the first several months? They can be quite demanding."

"Well, I only work part time so I'll be home for half of the week, and I've spoken to several sitters in the area. We've already looked at enrolling her in classes. I have a selection of toys and other items to help her feel welcome." I pull out the wicker basket I'd stuffed full of everything I thought Bella might enjoy.

"And her bed?"

"Here in the kitchen." Jake went ballistic when I suggested she could sleep with us. He doesn't show quite the same level of enthusiasm for Bella as I do. Seeing him with her caused my heart to swell and several other women to stop dead in their tracks and stare.

"You seem to be prepared. Have either of you owned a dog in

the past?"

"No, but we've read up on a lot of what Bella will need. We have the food she'll need to be on. The collar and lead have already been checked from our last visit." I start flapping about in the drawer I've designated as Bella's in the kitchen sideboard.

"Mrs...errr," Jake smiles at the woman and puts his arm around me to stop my fidgeting.

"Neville. Mrs. Neville."

"Mrs. Neville, as you can see, Lily and I are very serious about adopting Bella. We've got everything in hand and taken all of the advice we've already been given."

"Yes, it does look that way. Do you have any children? It's important if you have youngsters…"

"No." I cut in before she can continue. I look to Jake, and he comes to stand at my side. He slides his hand down my arm to engulf my hand. "We don't have children, and we don't have any plans for them in the immediate future." The last year hasn't been easy on either of us. We'd talked about the options open to us if we wanted to have a child but neither of us could or would agree. If we wanted, my eggs could be harvested, but I couldn't stand the thought of someone else carrying my child. It may be something I have to get over, but right now, I couldn't. Not even for Jake. He didn't want to adopt, stating we could still have our own child, and that's what he wanted—a child that was ours.

We both agreed we want a baby. We're just going to start with the furry kind.

"I must say, everything here looks good. There should be no reason why you can't pick Bella up when you're ready."

"Really?" I squeal.

"Really." She finally smiles, and she doesn't look so terrifying after all.

I turn to Jake. "We're going to get our baby." I jump up and wrap my arms around him.

"Yes, we are."

The End

ALSO BY RACHEL DE LUNE

The Evermore Series
More
Forever More
A Little Something More
Surrender to More
More Than Desire
Finally More

Cornwall Tides Series
New Tides

Standalone
Reminiscent Hearts
The Break

With Charlotte E. Hart
Innocent Eyes
Devious Eyes

ABOUT RACHEL DE LUNE

Rachel De Lune writes emotionally driven contemporary and erotic romance.

She began scribbling her stories in the pages of a notebook several years ago, and still can't resist putting pen to real paper. What ifs are turned into heartfelt stories of love where there will always be a HEA.

Rachel lives in the South West of England and daydreams about shoes with red soles, lingerie and chocolate. If she's not writing HEAs, she's probably reading them. She is a wife and has a beautiful daughter.

For every woman who's ever desired more.

Sign-up to her newsletter to receive
giveaways, news and exclusive excerpts
NEWSLETTER: http://eepurl.com/bckw0r
Visit her website
www.racheldelune.com

RACHEL ON SOCIAL MEDIA

facebook.com/racheldeluneauthor
instagram.com/racheldeluneauthor
twitter.com/Rachel_De_Lune
pinterest.com/RachelDelune
amazon.com/Rachel-De-Lune/e/B00ZS3RVKQ
bookbub.com/authors/rachel-de-lune

Printed in Poland
by Amazon Fulfillment
Poland Sp. z o.o., Wrocław